THE
LAST BLESSING
OF
J. GUYMAN LeGRAND

and Other Stories

DARIN COZZENS

ZARAHEMLA
BOOKS

The stories in this volume, some in much earlier versions, first appeared as follows:

"Chariot Race in D-Wing," *Sunstone*, Spring 2015.
"'Chopsticks' on the Ukulele," originally titled "Just Between God and Ferrill Ray," *Weber Studies*, Vol. 14, No. 2 (Spring/Summer 1997).
"The Last Blessing of J. Guyman LeGrand," *Irreantum*, Vol. 13, No. 2 (2011).
"Liquidating Earl Haws," originally titled "Tourniquet," *Greensboro Review*, No. 39 (Winter 1985–86).
"Sky-Loft Lovelies," originally titled "Doyle's Policy," *New Mexico Humanities Review*, No. 34 (1991).
"Spinsters and Their Dreams," originally titled "Wooden Rifle," *Waugh Street Journal*, Vol. 6 (Nov. 1993).
"Turtle Feathers," originally titled "Year of the Emu," *River Oak Review*, No. 18 (Spring 2002).
"The Washtub," originally titled "The Auction," *Inscape*, Fall 1984.

Cover designed by Jason Robinson
Design and layout by Marny K. Parkin

ISBN 978-0-9883233-9-1

Printed in the U.S.A.

Published by:
Zarahemla Books
869 East 2680 North
Provo, UT 84604
info@zarahemlabooks.com
ZarahemlaBooks.com

"This gathering of eight stories is first rate. As much a novel as a story collection, these fictions are united by milieu, by the gritty reality of rural farming life, and by the characters who appear in more than one story. More than anything else, they are united by Mormonism as culture and faith. There is humor in some characters' eccentricity and pathos in the moral striving of others, made persuasive by the particularity of presentation. The ultimate accomplishment here is the rendering of a world-in-small not to be forgotten by serious readers."

—Gordon Weaver, winner of two Pushcart Prizes and the O. Henry Award, author of ten short-story collections and four novels, including *Count a Lonely Cadence*

"Put them all together and they spell 'Balford,' these strong stories by Darin Cozzens. Balford is a Mormon community of strivers and hopers, farmers and dreamers, wives and patriarchs. The narratives are as sturdy as sawhorses, yet they are animated by quirky, earnest, genuine personalities. *The Last Blessing of J. Guyman LeGrand* is a rare and invaluable accomplishment."

—Fred Chappell, novelist and poet laureate of North Carolina from 1997 to 2002

"Darin Cozzens' writerly skill and unmistakable voice make the stories in this book more than just tales of rural Mormon life. Although Balford, Wyoming—the town at the center of this collection—is small, the characters portrayed and themes explored are anything but insignificant. The characters' relationship to the land and to one another anchor each story in the universal themes of longing, love, and the search for truth and meaning. There is humor in Cozzens' work, but more than anything there is yearning, heartbreak, and the tantalizing hope for connection and redemption. This collection deserves a readership as wide as the Wyoming sky."

—Angela Hallstrom, author of the novel *Bound on Earth* and editor of *Dispensation: Latter-Day Fiction*

"These are first-rate stories. They show how Mormonism works in everyday life. More, they reveal how human Mormons are, in spite of their faith, or, perhaps more to the point, because of it. The conflicts, characters, and settings are real. The stories fulfill two requirements of realistic fiction beautifully: to teach and entertain. Cozzens writes skillful prose, never wastes a word, holds the reader's attention with every line. The collection is a very welcome addition to Mormon fiction."

—Douglas Thayer, author of *Hooligan* and *The Tree House*

To my mother,
Vesa Adams Cozzens

CONTENTS

"CHOPSTICKS" ON THE UKULELE

I T WOULDN'T HAVE SURPRISED ME ONE LITTLE BIT IF Patty Dew had snatched Valentine's Day right out from under me, after all my months of planning. The only reason she settled for the middle of January was because she's starting to show. That was her parents' one and only New Year's resolution for 1958: Get Patty Dew married this time. And boy, did they! That's all Big Frett talked about in testimony meeting today was the "grand nuptial celebration" two weeks ago for his little girl.

At home, after supper, I told Daddy I had fully intended to get up and say something about my own wedding—which is only twelve days away now. I wanted to say how thankful I am that Heath Haymore is worthy to take me to the temple; like most Mormon girls, that's where I've always wanted to get married. But after Big Frett went on so long about the big wedding celebration at his big house, anything I might've said about the temple wouldn't have compared. From the kitchen, Mother overheard me and said, "Sour grapes does not become you, Fonda Penroy."

I know Patty's the baby and all that. And after nine boys, I suppose a father's got a right to dote on his only daughter. But the way Big Frett carried on, you'd think she'd married the Duke of York instead of Winn Bingham. Winn Bingham might have showed up for the ceremony—which is more than the first groom did, I admit—but people don't call him *Wild* Winn for nothing.

And is it sour grapes to be just a little tired of Big Frett's testimonies in general? Every first Sunday of my life, after the sacrament, the bishop says to the congregation, "The time is now yours to come forward as you feel prompted," and guess who's always first to the podium? When I was a girl, I used to imitate Big Frett, could make my older sister Faye laugh until she cried. I know the name is more to help folks keep him and Frett Jr. straight, but he really is a *big* guy, grabs the podium with both hands, like he's getting ready to yank it loose. My dear brothers and sisters of the Balford Ward! I would indeed be remiss if I didn't stand on my feet this day and thank the Lord for the plenitude of my blessings! Then for the umpteenth time we have to hear about that manna-from-heaven government contract for electric poles during the Depression; then hitting oil in every gopher hole in Elk Basin right after the war; then, during the Fifties, it's been the banking and real estate boom. It's not like Big Frett *never* mentions faith in the Savior and forgiveness and living prophets and the truthfulness of the Church—what a testimony is usually about—but the bulk of it goes to his plenitude.

One time Mother caught me in the middle of a performance. "Mockery does not become you, Fonda Penroy." She and Big Frett are second cousins. Besides his wife Bernene, who was a Vanderfisk (and who is no small specimen herself), my mother's the only other person I know who calls him Arthur. But this family connection with Cousin Edrus is not something he ever acknowledges in public. Put it this way: He married money; she married Crufford Penroy.

And don't get Big Frett started on his kids. He's been known to stop in the middle of his testimony and invite the whole litter to come up from their front pew and join him. He lines them up between the podium and the organ, always makes sure the twins are side by side. Nobody else in the Balford Ward, maybe in the whole Church, would do such a thing during testimony meeting. He calls them the ten tribes of Maxwell. You ought to hear him. This, my brothers and sisters, is the *real* wealth in life, the *real* bounty from on high! He puts Patty Dew right in the center. Isn't she beautiful? Isn't she lovely? A flower among weeds. A rose among thorns. He *says* that, but everybody knows he thinks the boys are paragons, too.

The last time he did the posterity line-up was when Merrill and Ferrill got back from Korea. And he did it before that when Bruce miraculously made it home from Iwo Jima in one piece. But the first posterity line-up ever was when Patty was a baby, on the very day she was blessed and given a name in front of the congregation. After the blessing, Big Frett held her up at the podium in her little white dress and bonnet so everybody could ooh and ah. That's when he said he really thought, with the birth of Frett Jr. four years earlier, that his quiver might have to be full of righteous sons only. But then the Lord had seen fit to send him and Bernene a precious daughter. This was the first Sunday of February, 1940. I remember because she was born on my birthday, January 15, and I had just turned six. I also remember asking Mother, right after the closing hymn and benediction, what a quiver was.

The meeting was over. People were already standing up and chatting, so nobody heard me. Nevertheless, she shushed me, told me in her hiss of a whisper to wait and ask Daddy someday when I got a little older. She had the same answer in testimony meetings after that, when I asked about Big Frett's references to multiplying and replenishing the earth and fruit of the loins. She's always been what you might call painfully uncomfortable with anything even close to the subject.

Or she is with me, anyway. When I read her the part of Heath's letter about reserving a honeymoon suite in West Yellowstone—which is only two hours from the Idaho Falls temple—it was the perfect opportunity for whatever a mother might want to say to a daughter about what to expect on her wedding night. And what do *I* get? Excruciating embarrassment and dead silence. I know she was only sixteen when she was a bride. I know it was hard. But with Faye married and gone, who else am I going to ask such things? When she finally does say something, it's just another warning that Heath Haymore could back out at any moment. And behind that warning there's always the little hint that she's half surprised he hasn't.

But in Mother's case there is another reason for reacting so strangely to anything related to the Maxwells' fertility. For years of testimony meetings and plenitude, there she sat, wanting another baby worse than anything. But after me, no more babies came—at least not until I was almost twenty. By then little Hewell was as much a shock as a miracle.

Sometimes I wonder if trying so hard in those twenty years ever got to be like, I don't know, a *chore*. Honestly, with Mother and Daddy, it's almost impossible to feature it being anything *but* a chore. By the time she finally got pregnant, I was away at college. But that's one time I really would've liked to be home, when she broke the news. I can see Daddy sitting one morning over his mush and toast while she goes ahead and shells his boiled eggs for him. When she sets them in front of him, peeled and shiny, he's bound to ask what's the occasion. That's when she gets this peculiar smile on her face and says, "Crue, you're not going to believe this."

Big Frett would have done a posterity line-up again today, I'm pretty sure, except Patty Dew's not back yet from her honeymoon. Which was another topic for him—how the happy couple is due home soon from Florida to face a very bright future together. Bright future? From what I hear, Winn Bingham has neglected his poor widowed mother's farm to the brink of foreclosure. That's just one of several things conveniently *not* mentioned in the testimony—that and how Daddy prevented disaster at the most hastily cooked-up nuptial celebration in history.

When I heard Patty Dew was all of a sudden getting married— I'm talking about the *first* wedding date, in mid-December—it was no big surprise. She has never hurt for male admirers. She has the perfect face and figure. I admit it. For garnish, you might say, she somehow always forgets to fasten the next button up on those paper-thin blouses of hers. Even when she was a little girl, folks bragged on her looks, said she was going to have to fight the boys off with a stick.

But it's more than just pretty. She's talented and lively and delightful. She really is charming. There's no other word for it. At a ward harvest supper and talent show the year before I went away to college, she sang "I Love You for Sentimental Reasons." The performance was mesmerizing. For the four or five minutes this eleven-year-old girl was singing, the people of the Balford Ward weren't sitting around folding tables in a church gym looking at the last of their spaghetti casserole and apple crumb. They were somewhere else. After that, my flute solo of "Come Thou Fount of Every Blessing" might as well have been "Chopsticks" on the ukulele. Even Daddy praised her. "Say what you want about Big Frett," he said on the way home, "but that girl's got some vocal chords."

Nobody ever said anything like that about me. And boys? Well, I went on a few dates at Ricks College, but to be honest, I've spent a lot of Friday nights alone, especially in those three years between graduating and meeting Heath Haymore. It's not easy being out of college and single in a place like Balford. With my secretarial degree, I got a job soon enough at Woolworth's in Cody, but everywhere you go, it's like you've got OLD MAID stamped across your forehead. And my mother might as well have done the stamping. She kept after me to go to Young Adult firesides and dances even when I told her how I felt at those things with all the kids fresh out of high school. "Party pooper," she said. "You think your older sister found herself a fella by moping at home?"

Mother forgets. The firesides and dances around here had nothing to do with Faye finding somebody. And she forgets that she didn't approve of Dwaine Tidwell at first anymore than she approves of Heath. For one thing, they both happen to be from Idaho, which is somehow an affront to her. "What's wrong with the boys from Balford?" Mother wanted to know.

What's wrong with the boys from Balford, at least in my case, is they never showed a lick of interest.

Patty Dew had the opposite problem. But maybe it wasn't such a great problem to have after all. What I heard was the father is some University of Wyoming football player she met last summer when she was visiting her brother in Laramie. Frett Jr.'s been going to school down there since he got home from his mission in Japan. Patty had just graduated from high school, but she goes out two or three times with this football player who's not the least bit religious, let alone Mormon, and all of a sudden she changes her mind about Ricks and decides to go to college at UW. Maybe by then something had already happened. But what for sure got her in trouble must have been sometime in October. I mean, do the math.

If anybody can put a good face on a daughter's out-of-wedlock pregnancy, it's Big Frett. But even he didn't try that for the December ceremony, the one that never came to pass. It was all hush-hush. Patty didn't finish the term at the university. She came home on the bus and then went right back to Laramie in the family Chrysler, straight to the office of the Albany County Justice of the Peace. But none of them banked on the groom not showing.

One side of me felt like it served her right. How many times in our growing up did Mother warn me and Faye not to flirt and flaunt, to keep both feet on the ground and hands to ourselves? But then the other side of me hears my mother's voice bringing up even more things that do not become me, like pettiness and resentment and self-righteousness. And in this case, I couldn't argue much. It's not all Patty's fault. I know that. As far as the football player, it *is* pretty bad to skip out on a girl you've done that to and hightail it back to Kansas City or St. Louis or wherever he was from. Heath Haymore and I don't *have* to get married—except now I've got the dress and have sent out announcements and everything—but even so, if he left me high and dry on our wedding day, I'd hunt him down.

So I felt bad for Patty; I did. The one I didn't feel so bad for was her dad. On that first Sunday of the new year, I was actually looking forward to a break from his testimonies. And for just a little while, I thought I was going to get it. I mean, what is there for a guy like Big Frett to say when life *isn't* rigged in his favor? For the first time in who knows how long, when the bishop invited ward members to come forward as they felt prompted, there was no movement from the front pew. All for the best, I thought. Big Frett's place was right there beside his daughter, for comfort and support in her hour of reproach.

But he fooled me. He was just waiting to be the *last* testimony. That's when he stands up and announces, to everyone's amazement, that Patty Dew's getting married after all. Only he didn't say "after all." In fact, from what he said, you would never have known there'd been a first wedding date. He spoke as if Patty and Winn Bingham had been betrothed to one another from birth.

While Big Frett waxed eloquent, I wasn't the only one to sneak a peek at the widow Etha Bingham on her pew, wondering what she felt about all this. But her face was a mask—no smile, no frown, no nothing. The whole thing was strange. Not so long ago, before the pregnancy anyway, Patty wouldn't have given Winn Bingham the time of day. And why would somebody like Wild Winn suddenly decide to marry a girl twelve years younger than he is and already two or three months along with some other guy's baby? So when did he agree to the deal? After the new pickup and tractor? There wasn't an ounce of romance in any of it. But then, what kind of feeling could you really expect between somebody jilted and somebody bribed?

All I know is Big Frett drastically changed his approach to this wedding. Since keeping it secret in December was evidently a jinx, this one in January was going to be Balford's version of a princess's ball. And the Maxwells wanted the whole town to know it, starting with everybody in the Balford Ward. So during the closing hymn, after Big Frett sits down from his first testimony of the year, one twin makes his way to the left door of the chapel and the other to the right. And each has a stack of fancy invitations to hand out.

Mr. and Mrs. A. Frett Maxwell
request the pleasure of your company
in honoring the wedding of their daughter,
Patricia Dew,
and
Winn P. Bingham,
son of Mr. and Mrs. Arvis Bingham (husband deceased),
on Saturday, the eighteenth day of January,
nineteen hundred and fifty-eight,
at 109 Balford Hill.
Buffet dinner at four o'clock
to be followed by a grand nuptial celebration.

"Under the circumstances," as Bishop Sebright instructed, the actual wedding ceremony was kept small and private and taken care of earlier that afternoon in the living room. But probably to keep peace with Bernene, he didn't put any limitations on the reception. If only out of curiosity, you have to go to something like that.

By late afternoon of the chosen day, it was bitterly cold. Sitting in Daddy's pickup for the fifteen miles from our farm to Balford Hill, with frost thick on all the windows, felt like sitting in an igloo. Mother was holding the wedding gift—kitchen towels and crocheted pot holders wrapped in pretty silver paper (left over from Christmas)—and dodging the gearshift. Hewell, who has to be the heaviest four-year-old on earth, was sitting half on her lap and half on mine, and I was pressed against the door so hard I was afraid it was going to fly open at every turn. It's got a bad latch.

But Daddy couldn't worry about that. Leaning over the steering wheel, he strained to see the road through one saucer-size hole in the windshield frost. He had to keep pushing the front flap of his ratty trapper hat out of his eyes and de-fogging with a yellow cloth work glove. We were lucky not to wreck going through town and even luckier not to smash into the cars parked everywhere around Big Frett's giant house and tennis court and fancy mule barn—especially with all the turning and weaving, hunting someplace to park ourselves. The maneuvering was even more complicated than it would have been because we were towing Daddy's old steel-wheeled bean wagon loaded with forty bales of barley straw. He planned to stop by the LeGrands' house, after the whole nuptial party thing, and stack the straw against the foundation, to insulate the crawl space.

"Maybe closer to the pond," Daddy said, more to himself than to anybody else, grunting every time he moved his arms to steer. "There won't be anybody down there." It wasn't just the full cab crowding his elbow room; he was wearing his patched-up denim barn coat over his Sunday suit, and it was a tight fit.

And that's when Mother said, "Honestly, Crue, I don't know why you had to trail that contraption along, today of all days. The straw could've waited."

"Till when, Edrus? It's going to get down to twenty below zero tonight. You want the stake patriarch's pipes to freeze?"

"You could've at least put the straw in the truck, and we wouldn't have needed to go racketing through town, every eye in Balford staring at us."

"Since when did you get uppity about my wagon?"

This was the bean wagon Big Frett had actually come out and looked at when he was first in the market for something to pull behind his prize mules, something to show off in parades and political campaigns. *Don't fret over your children's education! Vote Big Frett Maxwell for the school board!* But it was clear right away he didn't see any possibilities in Daddy's rig. "Crue," he said, "I'm talking brass bands and floats, candy and balloons, Miss Park County waving pretty to the crowd. The only place you need to be pulling this thing is the dump."

I think that was the episode my parents must have had in mind as we looked for a place to park at Patty Dew's celebration. "I'm not uppity," Mother said, still dodging the gearshift. "Don't call me uppity."

Uppityness does not become you, Edrus Penroy.

When we finally got parked and out of the cab, we were next to the pond, just as Daddy had predicted. And the pond sat at the bottom of a long slope, below the main driveway, a pretty good hike from the house. But the location had its advantages. Down there, we could see things nobody else could see. All around the pond, liked numbers on a clock, were these stacks of logs and boards, crisscrossed for burning. And all around it, the drop-off at the bank was pretty steep, except for one spot, where the slope of the hill came down gradual right to the ice. And right there stood the two biggest stacks of wood, way higher than my head. They looked like a gateway onto the frozen surface.

Daddy said, "The man must have a soft spot for fire."

Mother said, "And what's wrong with that?"

She motioned for me to take Hewell's other hand, and we set off toward the house, sort of dragging my little brother through ankle-deep snow. Without looking back, she told Daddy to bring the kitchen towels and potholders and be sure to leave the trapper hat and work coat in the truck.

"I'll freeze, Edrus."

"You're not going in that house up there looking and smelling like you just milked."

That's when I said it must be below zero already, even with the sun still up in the sky. Mother said it felt colder than that. And then Daddy, catching up with us, said he wondered how thick that pond ice was, because the water itself wasn't supposed to be all that deep.

He really did say that, which is sort of amazing when you consider what happened later.

When we got close to the big house, we smelled something good, and then out by the tennis court we saw a whole beef turning in a big brick roaster, over a bed of coals. Inside, the parlor and living room had been converted into a banquet hall. In one corner, they had a string quartet and, in the other, a gift table piled high. On a table next to that was the wedding cake, big as a wheelbarrow, with a little toy bride and groom framed in a heart on top.

And next to *that* were the newlyweds themselves, standing exactly like the toy couple, in this white pergola thing made of wicker and, yes, shaped like a heart! At least the top of it was. The heart wasn't closed at the bottom because the couple's feet had to go somewhere. It was cute. But you talk about awkward! Imagine Winn Bingham bathed and shaved, strangling in the buttoned collar and bow tie of a tuxedo, shaking hands with people who a week earlier would've called him worthless to his face. And everybody hugging Patty had to try not to stare at her midsection. At least Heath Haymore and I aren't complete strangers stuck with each other in a cake decoration.

The only problem with a grand nuptial celebration in Balford is lack of precedent. Nobody knew the exact agenda. But maybe Big Frett wanted it that way—one impressive surprise after another. This wasn't just punch and butter mints; this was a full roast beef-and-cheesecake feast. And, yes, lots of brides dance with their fathers—but accompanied by a string quartet?

And whereas most couples' special gift is a porch swing or bed linen, Winn and Patty's was a reservation brochure for a resort in Panama City, Florida. Judging by the gasps and hand-clapping, I wasn't the only one a little jealous at that point. I'm happy with West Yellowstone; I am. But to leave here twenty below zero and next thing you know be sitting on the beach with a warm breeze coming in off the Gulf of Mexico! That would be something.

Grand as everything was up to that point, I couldn't help wondering how the pond and all those piles of wood figured into the celebration. After the splendor of the Gulf of Mexico, I had about decided they didn't. It was early evening by now, almost dark outside, and the party had the feel of winding down. But then Big Frett climbs halfway up the parlor stairway and spreads his arms like Moses, to quiet everybody. But instead of bidding us a good night or offering a closing prayer, he says, "Friends, the moment has come to launch the bride and groom on their marriage journey."

So as it turns out, what had happened indoors was just half of what he had in mind.

Only a guy like Big Frett Maxwell could get people excited about going outside in below-zero weather and standing in the snow, which was pretty deep anywhere it hadn't been shoveled. But next thing you know, we're all bundled up, crowding around the parade wagon in front of the mule barn. The mules were hitched up and ready to go; you could see their breath. By then the sun had dropped behind Cedar Mountain, and a big yard light had come on, up under the eave of the barn. The wagon looked beautiful. It wasn't just the cold air and the electric light that made it so glossy apple-red. It had been completely repainted. The yellow letters on the sideboard and tailgate didn't say *Big Frett* anymore; now they said *Winn and Patty*.

But it *was* cold. Even in the hour and a half since our arrival, the temperature had dropped quite a bit. It was cold enough that when Daddy ran to the pickup for his barn coat and trapper hat, Mother didn't object. She was too busy massaging Hewell's hands through his little yarn mittens, trying to keep him from whimpering.

The front door of the house finally opened, and there they were—Winn P. Bingham, who obviously wanted to get all this over with, and his new wife Patty Maxwell holding on to his arm, more to keep from falling than anything else. They had coats on, but they were still in the tuxedo and dress. To everybody's surprise, Merrill and Ferrill came right along with them, carrying the heart-shaped pergola, trying to keep the couple centered in it. I heard Mother say, "My lands."

At the wagon, another brother was ready with a crate for a stepstool, and Frett Jr. was already standing in the bed to help haul the newlyweds up from the top end. As soon as they took their seat of honor on a bench bolted in the wagon bed, he tucked a blanket around their legs, hugged Patty Dew, and hopped out. Merrill and Ferrill in some way attached the pergola to the wagon's side panels and, presto, the couple's sitting in a heart!

Whether envy becomes me or not, that's what I felt, standing there frozen on Balford Hill. I can't deny it. Even with the out-of-wedlock pregnancy and the bribing, I had to admit that sitting inside that wicker heart, in a fancy wagon, *was* classy. Then, to crown it all, here comes Big Frett strutting out of the mule barn, wearing high black boots, a long-tail black coat and stovepipe hat, and holding a whip in one of his white leather gloves. He hauled himself up onto the driver's seat, took the reins, and hollered, "Let the grand nuptial march begin!" He touched the whip to the rump of each mule and said, "Get up, Buck! Let's go, Bonnie!"

If it wasn't already clear to the guests where Buck and Bonnie were taking the bride and groom, it got clear real fast when we heard *whoosh* and then *whoosh* again and turned to see two big fires way down the slope from us. No telling how much kerosene had been dumped on that wood. Then one by one, around the pond, the littler stacks flared up. You couldn't hear anything from the stacks on the far side, but just that fast the circle of bonfires lit up the pond and turned the dusk outside the circle into full darkness.

Daddy said, "Son of *a* gun."

By then Merrill and Ferrill and a few other brothers were herding us behind the parade wagon. It was getting colder by the minute. Mother was holding Hewell now, had him buttoned inside her own coat, and Daddy's earflaps didn't look all that silly. In fact, I had tied a scarf over my own ears. With each step down the slope those fires looked better and better. Besides the cold, the only snag so far in the grand nuptial journey was Buck and Bonnie being tempted astray by the barley straw on Daddy's old wagon, which was parked three or four little fires down from the gateway fires. Big Frett had to keep threatening with his whip and jerking them back in line.

At the edge of the frozen pond, not the least bit skittish, the mules actually stopped to nose the dead grass between the gateway flames. But the parade wagon was made for show, and standing still at the edge of the pond wasn't the show Big Frett had in mind. "Get up, mules!" he said, snapping his whip in the air. They clattered out on the ice, surefooted as could be. He couldn't have planned it any better. The same crusty snow as everywhere else made it hard for people to walk, breaking through every step, now kept hooves and wagon wheels from slipping. By the time everybody found a place around one of the big fires, it was easy to see what Big Frett was after. From any distance, the way the pond was lit up, the wagon looked like it was floating on air. It rolled along so smooth the bride and groom might as well have been riding in a pumpkin carriage. I know it sounds corny, but it wasn't. For the second time, I heard Mother say, "My lands."

About the time people started to get comfortable around the fires, holding their hands out and turning to warm their backsides, here comes another Maxwell son in a new four-wheel-drive pickup truck. In the front he's got Bernene with him, and in the back, lots of folding chairs and camp stools and a couple of long benches, not to mention two big insulated cans with spigots, and several covered trays that turned out to be loaded with cookies and doughnuts. It hadn't been all that long since dessert up in the house, but the cold seemed to give everybody a fresh appetite. People chattered and laughed, happy as could be, saying how the Maxwells sure know how to throw the grandest nuptial celebration they'd ever seen, as if there were plenty of such affairs in Balford to compare with. Drinking hot cocoa and eating doughnuts, you could hear the harness jingle and wheels creak, fainter and fainter as the nuptial wagon made the far half of its lap, then louder and louder on the near half.

After that first lap, the wagon drew up pretty close to one of the gateway fires. Poor Winn. Whatever his reputation, the guy looked forlorn. Or maybe the better way to say it is *resigned*. Either way, that's not exactly how you want a groom to look on his wedding night—at least not Heath, I hope. And the next item on the agenda didn't help. Winn's an only child, but before he knows what's hit him, the ten tribes of Maxwell are piling into the wagon to join the newlyweds for a family lap. With some help, arms boosting her arms and so on, even Bernene made it onboard. She sat right there on the driver's seat beside Big Frett, who was all smiles and waves. So the Maxwells—plus Winn—were in the wagon, and everybody else was around the fires. Without even thinking, I followed the wagon a little ways. I couldn't take my eyes off Patty in her heart-shaped pergola, kept wondering if it was too late for me and Heath to do anything even close to this. So I was the only one actually *standing* on the ice.

And then I felt something, and I don't mean envy this time. And heard something, too. The wagon was rolling along, forty feet away, but there was this funny groan and vibration under my feet. What came into my mind right then was the story in the *Balford Clarion* a few years back—two guys drowning while ice fishing at Yellowtail. Big Frett's pond isn't all *that* big around, and Daddy said it wasn't all that deep. But I got to wondering: Say I was up to my neck or even my waist—could I make it to the bank? In this weather? I looked at Mother, and Daddy standing beside her in his patched coat and trapper hat. He was drinking his cocoa from a paper cup and staring—not at me, but at the ice all around my feet. Did *he* hear something? I couldn't tell. I was really glad it was January and not early March. That's when those guys broke through at Yellowtail. It took divers a week to find them.

When the harness jingle got closer on the second lap, Daddy handed his cup to Mother and cut across the pond to meet the wagon. When Big Frett saw him, I heard "Whoa, mules," but that was all I caught of their conversation except for what was said just as he lifted his whip again: "It's ten below zero, Crue. You worry too much."

In a little bit the whole rig drew up beside the gateway fires again, and the weight of those mules and the parade wagon and the ten tribes of Maxwell bore down on the pond ice. Fire shadows flickered on the snow and on the bright red wagon and on people's faces. Daddy was still nervous. One of the mules had lifted his tail and left a big smelly pile steaming dark on the ice, but that's not what caught Daddy's eye.

Then I saw for myself. Creeping out from about the center of the gateway was a hairline crack.

Just as Daddy started toward the front of the wagon to say something again, Big Frett yelled, "One last lap! Anybody wants to wish the honeymooners well, hop on now or forever hold your peace!" Cold as it was, people pulled away from a blazing bonfire and swarmed the parade wagon. Not everybody, of course. Not the Widow Bingham, or Bishop Sebright and his wife, or Mother and Hewell. Or Daddy. And a few of the Maxwell boys and their wives got *off* the wagon, not to mention Bernene herself, which of course lightened the load quite a bit. But there were plenty of others to take their places.

"All aboard!" Big Frett yelled. Every time somebody climbed on—there must have been twenty people in the bed of that wagon, hanging on wherever and however—I thought I heard that groan again. Though with the jostling of the wagon and the mules lifting and setting down their hooves, eager to be moving, it was hard to tell. And at that particular moment, the little crack in the ice didn't seem to be getting any longer. Big Frett touched his whip to a mule's rump one last time and said, "Let's go, Buck! You, too, Bonnie!"

I don't remember exactly the order of things from there. Daddy was standing with one hand on the tailgate, like he was pushing, trying to hurry the loaded rig on its way. I know this: I was really glad he was there on the ice with me. The wagon lurched forward, like normal, but after a few feet, it began to sag—I don't know how else to describe it—like it was rolling to the center of a trampoline. Because the *ice* was sagging. I kept my eyes on one spoke, followed it around and around a few times before I realized I was standing in slush. Water was bubbling up from somewhere and soaking the snow. And then Daddy shouted, "Watch out!" and lunged to grab my hand. In the process, his feet made a splash and got my face all wet, but he's the only reason I made it back up on ice that *wasn't* sagging. Somewhere in all that, Big Frett turned around—probably to tell Daddy to pipe down—and there was a *big* groan and then a splintering noise, and the ice that was sagging like a bowl went ahead and broke all to pieces. When that happened, the wagon's back wheels dropped as if a trap door had gone out from under them.

For a second before the mules broke through up front, people in the wagon were swaying and tottering and flailing, holding to each other and fighting for balance; it's a wonder nobody went overboard headfirst. And there was Big Frett fighting the reins and looking backwards, the stovepipe hat and testimony face framed in the most bizarre way in that wicker heart.

Soon enough the parade wagon had settled and was standing level, up to its tailgate in icy water. You could still see the top half of the yellow-painted *Winn and Patty*. So the pond wasn't *deadly* deep, but deep enough, with the cold water flooding in, to scare a load of people crammed into the bed. Once they got over the scare, though, and were sure the wheels had found bottom, they started laughing and carrying on.

Big Frett had his hands full with the mules. They were in what must have been a sort of low spot in the pond floor, up to their withers and floundering pretty bad. He kept hauling on the brake and crying, "Whoa, Buck! Whoa, Bonnie!" Tails, manes, hair, harness—everything was glazed with ice. As long he could keep the mules calm and keep the wagon from inching deeper into the low spot, folks could maybe somehow get back on the bank and by the fire.

But that was the problem. Besides the ice broken up all around it, the wagon was too far from the bank for jumping, maybe twenty feet or so, and too deep for wading in such weather after all, as Frett Jr. found out. He had stayed on the wagon for the last lap and now got it in his head that making it to shore was somehow going to help the situation. But from the instant he jumped into the water, he couldn't find his feet. If Daddy hadn't thrown him a rope right away—he had one in his toolbox—one of the other brothers would've gone in after him and made two to have to rescue. When they finally dragged Frett Jr. out, he was already shivering so bad he couldn't talk.

All this time Bernene was busy being frantic. "Are you all right, Sweetie?" she yelled. Right then you couldn't tell if she was talking to Frett Jr. or Patty Dew or her husband. "Don't be scared. Hang on! Just hang on!" Then all of a sudden you *could* tell. "Arthur! Arthur! I think Buck and Bonnie are going in deeper. Is it too deep, Arthur?" The strange thing was, hauling Frett Jr. out—which got Daddy wet himself—and over to the fire just made the whole situation seem more hopeless. That twenty feet of icy pond water might as well have been the Bering Strait.

The parade wagon is a lovely showpiece, but that's all it is. At something like a church potato digging or apple picking, anybody lugging a sack or bucket toward Big Frett's rig gets pointed to Daddy's or somebody else's. Sitting high on his shiny red seat, looking ridiculous in bib overalls and penny loafers, Big Frett explains by saying, "Let's not scratch the paint on this one, brother."

Well, his shiny paint didn't count for much the night of the grand nuptial celebration. And for once it wasn't his wagon that people will remember. Before Daddy's headlights even came on, his pickup was roaring toward the big bonfires, everybody scattering out of the way. He made a wide swing, like he was going to the house. Then he stopped hard and jammed the truck in reverse. If you know anything about wagons, you know they don't back up very well, at least not for very far. But Daddy didn't have very far to go. Just to the edge of the slope, between the gateway fires—plus twenty feet. He didn't brake or clutch; he just backed his wagon into the pond, banging it hard through ice chunks, and he didn't stop until the truck's back tires rolled in up to their lug nuts in water. That put his wagon's tailgate within a hop of Big Frett's sideboard.

Daddy got out of the truck and grabbed a crowbar from his toolbox. He moved around to his back bumper, stepped onto the wagon's pipe tongue, and walked it like a tightrope. No matter that the tongue was treacherously icy under the soles of his Sunday shoes, or that it slanted downward into water he was going to have to wade through, or that several balls of mule manure happened to be floating right there. He sloshed through, in Sunday socks and pants already wet from rescuing Frett Jr., then climbed up the front of the wagon. No matter that when he got home he'd spend the rest of the night by the stove coaxing feeling back into his feet. For now, he crowbarred off two of his own sideboards, laid them between the wagons as a bridge, and got Merrill and Ferrill busy helping people cross over. Then Daddy dropped a bale of oat straw between his wagon and the pickup bumper—then another and another. There was nothing panicky or haphazard about it. He dropped those bales so they landed tight as puzzle pieces. One layer of bales sunk in and sponged up water first thing, but the layer on top of that made a bridge to dry ground.

Meanwhile, Big Frett was sawing pretty desperately on the reins.

"Aren't the mules going in too deep, Arthur? Aren't they?"

The same time Daddy crowbarred his sideboards—pulled the bolt heads right through the original holes—Wild Winn Bingham stood up from the newlywed bench and tore off his tuxedo bowtie. He wrapped his share of blanket around his new bride and turned her so she was sitting sideways in the heart-shaped pergola, with her feet up on the bench and out of the water. Then he told his new brother-in-law Ferrill to pass him a bale of straw. Winn broke it open and wedged a fat flake under his arm. Next thing you know he's crawling past Big Frett on the driver's seat, soft-talking the mules the whole time. Even with everything icy glazed, he somehow got astride the one on the left and leaned like he had a secret to whisper in one of those big ears. Then he went to petting and soothing both of them, and feeding them mouthfuls of barley straw. He did all this with ice chunks bumping his knees.

People were moving steady across the two bridges, one made of wood, one made of straw, both of them put together by my daddy. Mother was there by the pickup bumper, with four or five others, reaching and steadying, saying, "Watch it. Just a little farther. There you go." As the wagon passengers made it to the bank, one by one, the rescuers kept reminding them that either big fire was just a step away, like they couldn't see it for themselves, and that there was plenty of hot cocoa left. One of the Maxwell brothers had just come from the house, again, this time with towels and blankets.

Since Winn had the mules under control, Big Frett tied off the reins and clambered backwards over the seat to help the twins get Patty Dew down. She was the last one. She was still sitting with her feet on the bench, inside the wicker heart, holding the hem of her dress in one hand. "It's just a gown, Sweetie!" Bernene shouted.

The way it worked out, Big Frett stood on the straw bridge, holding out his arms while the twins helped Patty find footholds down the front of Daddy's wagon. "It's all right, Honey," Big Frett kept saying. She was doing fine on her own, but all of a sudden he reached for her like you would a child climbing somewhere dangerous or off-limits, and kind of pulled her away from the wagon and cradled her in his arms. It was like he couldn't help himself. Somewhere in that process the stovepipe hat fell into the water, right where those mule balls were floating. He didn't even notice. "I got you now," he said. "I got you, Patty Dew." And Big Frett, all two hundred and eighty pounds of him, carried his daughter bride the last of the way across the straw bridge without even a hint of a stumble. And when he took the last step to dry ground, it wasn't Bernene who got to the bride first to wrap her in a blanket and hug her and say sweet things to her. It was my mother.

Even in the flickering light I could tell Patty had been crying. And not because of the ruined nuptial celebration, which is what everybody else probably thought. Even with six years' difference between us, and my wedding still a couple of weeks off, I knew she was crying because she was too *young* for all that had happened to her, for what was *going* to happen to her. Did she look at Winn Bingham out there in his frozen wet tuxedo and see a husband or just some guy steadying a team of mules and tying one end of a line to the wagon's doubletree while my daddy tied the other to the back bumper of the Maxwells' four-wheel-drive? Did she have any idea how cold those toes of his were going to be in some motel bed between here and the beach resort in Florida? I knew Mother was thinking the same thing because that's when she came up to me, with tears in her eyes and a strange look on her face, and said, "It'll all work out, Fonda."

Heath Haymore and I have kept our feet on the ground and hands off each other, but I have wondered why nobody ever tells you the excitement is half fear. Love is a fearful thing. Between husband and wife, between parent and child. That's the truth of it. I love Heath; I do. And in twelve days I'm going to marry him. But ever since Patty's wedding, I've had this nagging feeling that, Valentine's Day or not, until you've lived some of what marriage puts you through, maybe love isn't even the right word.

THE WASHTUB

I.

Speer Newman

Last thing last night, the washtub had been where it needed to be, where Mrs. Sebright had finally agreed to let it be—at the bottom end of the third row, on a plywood-and-sawhorse table in company with a scythe, a pair of hames, and a two-man cross-cut saw. But at 11:40 on this cold Saturday morning in late February of 1987, only twenty minutes before the auction was to begin, it was back at the top of the first row—sitting forlornly on the frozen ground of the hay yard, between a World War II–era high chair and crib. It was hard not to admire such defiance. Still, his five years in auctioneering had proven well enough that the difference between collectible and junk was sometimes nothing more profound than association.

"Any horse dealer can tell you, Mrs. Sebright: You don't want to market your prize mule with the donkeys."

"I don't have a mule," she had said.

Eileen Sebright

As recently as last night, she had expected to equate a good turn-out with neighborliness and affection. Yet now that cars and trucks were pulling into the field behind the house, parking one after another in uneven rows, she felt invaded. Doors swung open to release strangers in heavy coats and insulated coveralls.

Their voices and the vapor of their breathing intruded upon the stillness of the late morning's cold overcast.

Eileen closed the back door of the house and stood on the stoop to tie a wool scarf around her ears. Where no trail or passage ever before had been needed, auction comers now made one: across field stubble to the lilac hedge, past clothesline and pump house, between chicken coop and grain bins, then on to the hay yard—which, for the first time in thirty-eight years, held no hay.

She had suggested, for a display area, the unfenced lawn and adjoining garden plot, but Speer Newman wanted something more "enclosed," more "defined." What he wound up choosing was something just plain claustrophobic. The hay yard was bordered on one side by the empty corral's long, concrete feed bunk; and, on the other, by a string of sucker-rod panels one of the boys had welded in a shop class twenty years earlier. Both bunk and panel string angled into the windowless north wall of a calving shed. That angling shaped the yard like a funnel whose only opening at the narrow end was a single door in the shed's wall; and Roy had wired its latch shut to discourage wandering. Short of retracing their steps, people would be sort of trapped between rows, among all the goods up for auction.

"Yes, ma'am, that's the point," Speer Newman had said.

If he was contrary about location, he was even more so about arrangement. Not until such a juncture in a life did a person have to figure out what to do with all the stuff hauled from the familiar shelter of house and shop and outbuilding. She had favored a series of *short* rows, *across* the hay yard. So naturally Speer Newman ordered three *long* ones—a row on the left, parallel to the feed bunk; a row on the right, parallel to the sucker-rod panels; and a row down the middle. From one end to the other, those rows were at least forty yards long. The length made everything seem more exposed, more vulnerable.

"We'll tarp any of it you want tarped," Speer Newman had said last night, craning his neck to study the sky, "but there's no snow in those clouds."

Weather wasn't the threat Eileen had in mind. In place of yesterday's desire to present her earthly goods to fullest advantage, she now felt the urge to guard them against indecision and indifference. That urge had found its focus in the washtub. Why on earth would Speer Newman put such a thing on the very *last* table in that third row, where the panel fence ran into the shed? There was nothing in that corner except hay duff and ragweed stalks.

It belonged up in the first row, along the feed bunk, with the bulk of the household stuff. It was as much a part of raising her babies as the high chair and crib. When they moved on the place, the winter of 1949, the house didn't have a bathroom. She had just had Willard. She didn't remember, and didn't care, how all these years later the tub had come to be hanging from a spike inside the calving shed, alongside branding irons and a dehorner. Mules and donkeys! It hadn't always held warble repellant.

Roy was no help. He said to just go along with Speer Newman on the tub, that the man knew his business. But wasn't his business once farming, at least up until his wife died? Well, yes, Roy admitted. So shouldn't Speer Newman, of all people, know the difference between house and barn, and what goes where?

Harley

First thing this morning, Harley had reminded Speer, again, that he wanted to start doing more of the calling. As he spoke, he was looking at tractors and implements lined up in the pasture beyond the sucker-rod fence. Plow, disc, planter. Manure spreader, cultivator, sprayer. Swather, baler, combine. No matter that everything was worn out; it would still afford him some useful practice. After two years of working for A&A Auction, he was tired of gofering. When he hired on, he was satisfied with the understanding that he would fill in when Speer's vocal chords needed a rest. The problem with that agreement was that Speer's vocal chords had the durability of piano wire. So Harley got to ply his skills only when the boss granted himself a bathroom break or a quick sandwich, either of which was invariably timed so as to leave the understudy to coax bids on things like flower pots and tomato cages.

"Milk before meat, Harley." That's all Speer ever said.

All along Harley had clung to the conviction that the chances of advancement were better in a small outfit like A&A. Besides him, the only other employees (and the inspiration behind the company's name) were Speer's two daughters, both single and still going part-time to Cody Community College. The older one, April, was twenty-two and managed the registration table and receipts box. Autumn was only twenty, but she did all the clerking. They treated him like a kid brother still wet behind the ears. Which was a galling irony since he was twenty-five and already graduated from The Auctioneering School of America in Omaha, Nebraska.

Lately he had begun to worry about the pace of his advancement. He took full responsibility for squandering the first few years out of high school—as a bagger at Food Basket, then a patcher of flat tires at the Co-Op, then a parts man at Balford Auto. But those dead ends were behind him. The moment he saw the late-night TV ad for The Auctioneering School of America, the moment he called the toll-free number and enrolled in the next ten-week course of intense training, a new and urgent purpose came into his life. From start to finish, the training experience inspired him to grab life by the horns. That was one of many favorite sayings of a teacher named Captain Duke Fletcher, a retired fire chief with the city of Omaha. "It was a career-ending injury," Captain Duke said on the first day. "I could be watching talk shows and wasting away in Margaritaville right now, and drawing a mighty handsome disability for doing it." He had looked piercingly at the new auctioneering recruits. "But I said, 'Duke, you're better than that.' And I decided right then to pursue a brand new career and give something back!"

Captain Duke Fletcher was the closest thing to a role model Harley had ever had. "Em-u-la-tion," Captain Duke declared one day during a lesson on style. "It's the highest form of honor." Harley went right out and bought a ten-gallon hat and bolo tie, and decided it was time to try again on a mustache. After graduation, when he got home to his one-room apartment in Balford, he hung, with equal pride, two framed artifacts on his wall: the diploma certifying his new professional status and a photograph of him and Captain Duke.

When it became clear during the preliminaries of the Sebrights' auction that the grabbing of life by the horns would have to wait yet another day, Harley ventured a suggestion: Maybe today he could at least warm up the crowd. He was more than capable of clicking on the portable microphone, could easily imagine himself saying, with great authority, "Testing. One-two-three, testing." He could announce the location of the porta-johns (behind the barn) and point out the 4-H club's fundraiser table (under the awning of the machinery shed, beside the registration table). Why not let *him* push the coffee and hot chocolate and barbecue plates that would help send a group of deserving youngsters to their national convention in Kansas City? He even had a joke or two in mind—if Speer wanted to hear them.

"Maybe next time," Speer whispered. "And, Harley, see if you can sneak that tub back down the third row without Mrs. Sebright catching you."

Roy Sebright

Roy didn't have the heart, or the courage, to remind her of a detail from the tub's history that she evidently had blotted from memory—namely, how she couldn't wait to be rid of the thing. As soon as the bathtub had faucets and a drain, before the new bathroom's studs were even closed in, she declared she was ready to live in the twentieth century and never wanted to see that old washtub again. Yet her divestment had been his windfall. He liked that tub. It was ideal for working cattle. Resting on plank scaffolding beside the squeeze chute, it made a handy reservoir for whatever needed to be ladled down a heifer's spine, was big enough you didn't spend all your time mixing up a new batch.

The years had seen more spines than he could count. He had always thought his brood cow operation was the one consistent bright spot of his enterprise—until last fall, when the bank decided otherwise.

"Roy," Frett Maxwell Jr. had said when the last calves were sold, "your herd just isn't earning its keep anymore."

If you had to have a creditor—and Roy had never realized his dream of *not* having to have one—then let that creditor be Frett Maxwell Jr. He was fair, supportive, decent, unassuming; he was the same man behind a banker's desk as he had been, for a long stretch back in the Seventies, behind a bishop's desk at church.

Several of those qualities were not inherited from his father.

"Slopes and rocks is hardly what I'd call prime property," Big Frett Maxwell had said at the signing of the farm's original mortgage in the fall of 1948, when Frett Jr. was only twelve years old. "But," he added with a chuckle, "who am I to stand in the way of ambition? I just hope I live long enough to see you pay this off."

As a matter of fact, Big Frett didn't make it that far. At the time of his funeral a year earlier, the original thirty-year pay-off date had long since come and gone, extended by several debt roll-overs and, when crop and beef prices had found yet another bottom, a major refinancing.

Frett Jr. couldn't be here today to represent the bank, in his characteristic gesture of goodwill, so he was sending one of the loan officers under him. It was hard to keep the new ones straight. Roy had tractors older than most of them. From behind a far corner of the pump house, away from the lilac hedge and clothesline and steady stream of people, he watched the arrival of the last vehicles. Then, at three minutes to twelve, three minutes before he and Eileen were to stand with Speer Newman and be introduced, a sporty car turned off the highway and came racing down their lane. It took the curves and sinks much too fast. Just as heedlessly, it bumped across the field's entrance culvert, pulled onto the flattened stubble, and slid to a stop. When the door finally opened and the driver climbed out, Roy recognized the one bank delegate he hadn't figured on: the junior loan officer everybody called Cowboy Joe. By any common association, the name didn't fit. Instead of a truck, this cowboy drove a Camaro. And instead of a big hat and belt buckle and boots, he wore running shoes and a nylon warm-up suit. The only basis for the nickname was his fanatical allegiance to the University of Wyoming's sports teams and their mascot.

"People naturally think he's copy-catting *that* Cowboy Joe," Frett Maxwell had explained a few years back, referring to the pony paraded up and down the sideline at home football games. "But Joe's his real name. Joseph Oscar Leland. I'm the one who had to read his resumé."

Roy had seen his desk, the adding machine pushed to a far edge by fan-club mugs, shot glasses, insulated beverage cup, paperweight, pencils, pens, clips, caps. Cowboy Joe Leland was fond of saying that he bled brown and gold (which explained the Camaro's paint job and the two tones of his warm-up suit). The crowning devotion was the ceremonial gold pony blanket centered and draped over the back of the swivel chair so as to showcase the embroidered brown letters of the name.

Standing in frozen barley stubble, a long way from the junior loan officer precincts of the bank, this Joseph Oscar Leland donned a brown and gold coat, then a matching stocking cap, then a pair of matching gloves. Finally, he slipped something into one coat pocket—a pack of brown and gold chewing gum?—and something into another, locked his car doors with great vigilance, then made his way toward the lilacs lining the field's border ditch.

When Roy emerged from behind the pump house, Leland started, then quickly recovered.

"Hey, bud," he said, "I'm supposed to check in with the farmer. Sebright, I think his name is. Could you point me to him?"

Trudy Pruitt

Her Nashville client, Mr. Feinstein, wanted a bucksaw, but Trudy knew him well enough to know he could be persuaded of the customer appeal of its much bigger cousin. In her next phone call, she would help him envision the long two-man crosscut hanging over the mantel in his restaurant chain's newest location. In fact, she planned to recommend that an entire wall be devoted to a timbering theme. As it happened, much of the decor for such a wall—adze, double-bitted axe, peavey, maul, wedges— could be found in the hay yard of this little farm outside Balford. The top end of Park County was much farther north than she had planned to come, and much colder than expected. And she still had to get home to Denver tonight, a nine-hour drive even if the roads were clear. But what were more miles if they yielded good buys? On many long, lonely roads, she had learned how to stay awake—crushed ice and strictly rationed M&Ms. And with ski pants, ski gloves, a good parka and a knitted purple ear warmer, she was prepared for the weather.

Trudy Pruitt was thirty-seven, three years divorced, and childless. To say she was dedicated to her job was the thinnest of descriptions. She lived *by* and *for* what was known in some circles as procurement by proxy. Trudy Pruitt had a gift. Like Speer Newman, she knew the subtleties of association, knew how powerfully evocative ordinary objects could be. "You're not just peddling nostalgia like other companies peddle chic," she had told Mr. Feinstein. "You're touching people's soft spot."

"Whatever gets them in the door," he said.

Up to now on this week-long swing into Wyoming—to hit auctions in Laramie, Rawlins, Lander, Riverton—Trudy Pruitt had been disappointed. But thanks to the eleventh-hour discovery of a back-page, bottom-corner ad in a rolled-up *Shop and Swap*, her prospects had brightened. When she left Balford today, her mini-van would be loaded. On one plywood table in the second row, among trowels and floats, she immediately spotted a draw-knife and gimlet; on another, behind bottle jacks and tire irons, a shingle froe.

On her long drives, Trudy Pruitt often pondered choice and chance. So far, this day had favored the latter. The *Shop and Swap* was printed in Park County. Yet she found it stuck in the nozzle lever of a gasoline pump in Fremont County, a hundred and forty miles south of Balford, in the crossroads hamlet of Shoshoni. Except for a car cutting in front of her, she wouldn't have chosen that particular pump. And she didn't actually need gas to get to Casper, which should have been the next town on the way home; she just didn't want M&Ms to be the *only* reason for pulling into the Quick Stop.

And, too, there was the matter of her bidder number, assigned at the registration table under the awning of a machinery shed. A big *14* was written in thick marker, on a sturdy, saucer-sized paper plate glued to a tongue-depressor handle. Every time she waved that homemade number today, she would be reminded of the duration of her marriage.

Then the culminating coincidence:

"Oh, Ay-pril!" one of the 4-H fundraiser girls had called to the young lady at the registration table, "can we borrow your marker—since ours just died?"

Trudy Pruitt walked from the registration table back down the row on the right, toward the crosscut saw. She had always liked the name April, had never stopped hoping in fourteen years that her husband might be persuaded to fatherhood by the possibility of a baby girl.

At the end of the third row, something was different. The saw still rested on the plywood table, but at some point during the auctioneer's introducing of the farm couple and pointing out of the porta-johns and the first trilled chant of the day—*Let's-go-now, what'll-you-going-to give?*—saw and scythe and hames had been repositioned to accommodate a washtub. In Trudy Pruitt's line of work, old washtubs were not uncommon. But on this little farm in Balford, on this last Saturday in February of 1987, this one touched a soft spot in *her*. For a long time she stared. Only when a wadded gum wrapper sailed through the air and plinked off the tub's rim did she come to herself. Tracing the wad's arc, she found herself being watched by a guy in a brown and gold warm-up suit.

ll.

Harley

Halfway up the second row, during the bidding on a homemade garden cart with bicycle wheels, Speer's voice faltered. Harley was stunned, disappointed, delighted. The piano-wire vocal chords were fallible after all. He should have seen the moment coming. Over the past half hour—rakes, hoes, shovels, a hand spade and dibble—Speer's range had been flattening, and he had lost his panache. That's what Captain Duke Fletcher called it; Captain Duke maintained that without your own brand of panache, you were just another yodeler. But right now, panache was less a concern than basic competence. Several times Speer had tripped over himself, forgotten where he was with price increments, mismatched bid and bidder. At each stumble, Autumn looked up from her clipboard. Correction was as foreign to her as error was to him. Finally, when he made to announce the garden cart's new owner—"*Sold!* For . . . fifteen-fifty to number . . ."—he coughed and choked, tried mightily to clear his throat, ended up so hoarse he was unintelligible. Harley knew his boss, knew his habits and capacities. He could go for hours at a stretch, could plow through a warehouse full of heirlooms and relics, pallet by pallet, without hitch or tremble. His problem was not vocal fatigue.

After the garden cart, as the little crowd moved like liquid to encircle the next items for sale, Speer stepped for a moment out of the center of that crowd and drew close.

"Harley," he whispered with a strange anxiety, "I need you to do something for me."

Harley's veins burned with anticipation. The next items up for sale were a push mower, garden tiller, and a trimmer with a battered shaft. Hardly heavy field machinery, but a lot better than flower pots.

But Speer didn't want a break.

"See that number fourteen?" he whispered. "The lady with the purple—don't look! don't look!—do you see her?"

Harley saw her. At the beginning of the second row, she had bought a short length of log chain and had stayed with the pack ever since, snatching up anything related to timber. Her number had become so familiar she didn't even have to hold up the paper plate on the tongue-depressor handle. Her hair was pulled back in a pony tail, and her cheeks were colored from the cold. She was pretty.

Now Speer was furtive *and* embarrassed. "I need you to see what you can find out about her."

Harley chafed. A few worn-out pieces of garden equipment on a worn-out farm—what would it hurt to let him have *those*? But the chafing was countered by another feeling. In the two years he had worked for A&A Auction—two of the five his boss had been a widower—Harley had seldom seen him distracted, and never for the reason he was distracted today.

"What am I supposed to find out?"

"Find out . . ." Speer said, hesitating, then stalling. "What you need to know is . . . Oh, hell . . . What *I* need to know is"—he closed his eyes as if enduring the throb of a toothache or a bowel spasm—"just find out if there's a *Mr.* Purple Ear Warmer."

Harley's nod belied his utter absence of method or strategy.

"And, Harley," Speer said, his voice considerably recovered, "whatever you do, don't tell my daughters."

Cowboy Joe Leland

The sky hung low and gray, and the wind was picking up. Running shoes, which thus far had motivated no habit of running in Joe Leland's life, were the worst possible footwear for a day like this. Leland begrudged Saturday work of any kind, but auction duty above all. He hated farmer talk, the smell of tobacco, the tedium.

Bootjack. Step stool. Pair of lawn chairs. Laundry basket full of board games and Reader's Digest Condensed Books. A dozen glass-jug chick waterers. Sell them one at a time or as a lot? Please, please, please—as a lot. *Anything* to speed up the process.

Almost two hours into the thing, and the little cell of bidders and onlookers, with the auctioneer as nucleus, had barely cleared the second row. Their down-and-back pattern of movement put them once again at the wide end of the hay yard and Leland at the narrow end, maybe half a football field apart. From all the standing around and time-killing, his feet were clubs, even number than his hands. Still leaning against the calving shed, he unwrapped another stick of gum and checked his watch. It was 1:55. He patted the solid lump in the pocket of his brown and gold coat. Hope in the form of a radio and earplug. *Your voice of the Wyoming Cowboys!*

"I just do not get this," he had said yesterday afternoon to Frett Jr. "The stuff sells with or without us being there."

"The Sebrights have been with this bank a lot of years, Leland."

"What if I get somebody to cover for me?"

"We go through this every time," Frett had said. "What part of *your turn* don't you understand?"

"But it's a two o'clock tip-off—with Texas-El Paso!"

An hour per row. At this rate, it would be three o'clock before they even got to the junker machinery on the other side of the sucker-rod fence. Maybe *more* than an hour on this last row, because, right away, progress ground to a halt at six or eight crates of canning jars.

"Are they *all* wide-mouthed?" asked a fat lady in laceless work boots, yellow long-johns, and a corduroy skirt. She had a gravel maker of a voice, loud and masculine.

As always, Leland was dumbfounded by the dress and habits and concerns of auctiongoers.

The auctioneer turned to the old farm wife, who evidently was posted at the edge of the crowd for this very sort of question.

"How about it, Eileen?" the auctioneer asked.

Even with the portable microphone, the question was hard to hear, and not because of any deficiency in the auctioneer. After a spotty performance early in the second row, his voice had recovered—who knows how?—and was again confident, competent, diplomatically commanding. No, from where Leland stood, the problem was the breeze or air temperature or something, as was evident when the farm wife answered. As she spoke, she tugged her scarf tight and retied the knot beneath her chin. She didn't have the projection capacity of the fat lady in yellow long-johns, but she was no milquetoast. Her words just floated away. The crowd laughed long and hearty at what she had said, but the only thing Leland heard was a snatch about canning jars and donkeys.

After starting the whole fuss, the fat lady didn't even bid on the canning jars. When they finally sold, the crowd inched again toward the calving shed. Leland could see Roy Sebright standing by his wife, sharing the role of consultant. How many gallons in that sprayer tank, Roy? Horsepower from that motor? PSI generated by that compressor? And for every hose and cord, shaft and shank, bit and blade, the question was length. "That chainsaw's got a twenty-inch bar is what you told me, Roy, if I'm not mistaken?"

Patched denim coat and bib overalls, frayed trapper hat, grizzled whiskers. But old Roy was sharper than he looked and, two hours after the fact, was probably still relishing their first meeting, when junior loan officer Joe Leland might as well have jammed one of those size-twelve running shoes in his own mouth. *Could Old Sebright have picked a colder day to sell out? Since this is Sebright's auction—shouldn't he be a little easier to find? Between you, me, and the barn, I think an outfit like Balford Savings and Loan should've cut guys like Sebright loose a long time ago. What's his first name again? Rufe? Rafe? Roscoe?*

All the way to the hay yard, the old boy had let him go on and on, and never said a word. Only when the auctioneer singled the same old guy out of the crowd, invited him and his wife to stand beside the portable microphone, introduced him by name—only then did Leland realize his blunder.

If Frett found out, he'd have a fit. It wasn't the best time to test the limits of his patience, either. He was a nice old Mormon guy, pretty much immune to strong feeling of any sort, but after yesterday's grousing session about Saturday auction duty interfering with a basketball game, the look on his Mormon face had not been reassuring.

"Eight years you've been with us, Leland," Frett had said. "Do you ever wonder why you're still a *junior* loan officer?"

In that moment, they could have been in the house in Cheyenne instead of the bank in Balford, and Frett Jr. could have stood in for Joseph Leland Sr.: "Do you ever wonder why you're twenty-five and *still* don't have a bachelor's degree?" Did it ever cross his mind? Did it ever give him pause? "Do you think about this sort of thing at all, son—why you're twenty-seven and *still* don't have a real job?" On the occasion of the last question, Joseph Leland Sr. had laid out on the dining room table the advertisement for every entry-level banking position within a six-hundred-mile radius.

With luck, Frett might end up laughing at the Roy Sebright embarrassment: Sounds like Cowboy Joe got bucked off. And that wasn't the only time today. From his corner by the calving shed, as far from Roy Sebright as he could get, he had seen the woman with the purple ear warmer when she first approached, had said, "Got a thing for tubs?" But she was *all* business, hardly looked at him, and then didn't answer. Wedding ring? No telling with the ski gloves. If not married, she had to have a boyfriend; she wasn't bad looking. Whenever the bank hired a new teller, Leland made it a point to determine availability. It was helpful, a few years back, when his nickname spread beyond the men in the bank. It always prompted questions, which in turn provided a pretext for conversation. Before agreeing to a date, though, they always wanted more information. "No, seriously, who are you really?" And after a date or two—seldom more than that— they never called him Cowboy Joe again.

Though well preserved, the woman in the purple ear warmer had to be in her mid-thirties, which made the tellers seem even younger than they had begun to seem. For two hours, Leland had watched her. What she did have a thing for, obviously, was timbering tools. Maul, wedges, peavey, adze. But she had to be buying the stuff for somebody else; she didn't look like the lumber-Jane type. During stretches when nothing on her list was up for bid, she slipped away from the crowd, came just close enough to the calving shed to make sure the tub was still there, stayed just far enough away not to have to talk to him. She checked on the two-man crosscut saw, certainly, but it was the tub she kept eyeing.

And she wasn't the only one. The farmer's wife, Mrs. Sebright, had the same look on her face when she eased away from the cluster of bidders to study the tub. But one woman was seller, and one was buyer. And, judging by her single-mindedness, if Ms. Purple wanted that tub, there would be no stopping her—unless, for whatever reason, she couldn't deviate from timbering stuff. So what would happen if somebody bought it *for* her?

Leland stomped, swung his arms, jumped up and down a few times. But suppose Mrs. Sebright wanted the tub back and, out of seller's embarrassment, just wasn't telling anybody? She would have to smile kindly on the person who restored it to her. And if *she* smiled kindly, her husband couldn't hold too much of a grudge. And if he didn't hold a grudge, maybe anything that got back to Frett would be positive, maybe even commendatory. *Do you know what that nice junior loan officer did for me?*

Leland looked at the crowd creeping his way. Slow as molasses. Slow as amoeba. He was cold and hungry. Those 4-H barbecue plates were still selling and were starting to smell pretty good. That's when he thought to check his watch again: 2:07. He had missed the tip-off.

Speer Newman

There was no Mr. Purple Ear Warmer.

"How did you find out?" Speer asked.

"That one in yellow long johns—she's a buyer, too. Autumn pointed her out."

"I told you not to say any—"

"I didn't," Harley said, "not to Autumn. But it turns out Long Johns knows Fourteen, *personally.*"

So. Her name was Trudy Pruitt, she bought mostly for restaurant chains, was from Denver, probably somewhere in her midthirties, *and* she was several years divorced. Working the third row—digging bars, crowbars, wrecking bars, gallon cans of nails and bolts, buckets of pipe fittings, a thousand oddments of hardware—Speer almost regretted the thoroughness of the profile. Where there was no charm to fall back on, he would have to rely on conversation. And, despite the vocal demands of his adopted profession, conversation did not come easily.

In contrast, it had been one of his wife's many gifts. At the funeral, the eulogist had said so. Sitting between his daughters on the front pew of Ralston's little First Methodist Church, not five feet from the bier, listening to the cataloging of those gifts, Speer had found no seam between grief and guilt. At the time, he was not quite forty-one. The bier's four wheels framed the same square of carpet where, eighteen years earlier, he had faced her, upright and alive, where they were pronounced man and wife.

"So what are your plans?" someone had asked between bites of wedding cake in the fellowship hall.

"*He* wants to farm," she had said.

At the time of their wedding, mid-September 1964, she would have supported any alternative. After a few years, latent support turned into active suggestion and, after a few more, into subtle insistence. Accounting. Retail management. Law enforcement. Natural gas furnace installation and servicing. Horseshoeing. She brought home brochures on a dozen job training programs from newly founded Cody Community College. But every time she pushed, he balked. That difference was the thorn of their marriage. The doctor said brain aneurysms were freaks of the vascular system, as unpredictable at age eighty-nine as thirty-nine. "Stress has nothing to do with them," he said.

Speer didn't believe him. A week after the funeral—mid-September, with half the harvest still in the field—he put his place up for sale and called the number on the last brochure his wife had brought home, this one for a six-week course in auctioneering, to begin the first of November.

"I love you, Daddy," April had said, "but why do this *now*?"

Because decisiveness was penance.

According to Harley, Trudy Pruitt was interested in the wash-tub, which didn't at all seem to fit her buy-list. So what if some-body bought it *for* her and made a gift of it? No sooner had Speer set that question to simmer than he caught another glimpse of Mrs. Sebright. She was still bitter about the final relocation of the tub. He *had* been cavalier, and every bit as sneaky as she was. But she had the better right to be proprietary: It was her tub and maybe should remain so.

Trudy Pruitt or Mrs. Sebright?

Decisiveness was penance.

Roy Sebright

Just past the sausage grinder with a bad electric cord sat a brooder lamp with no cord at all.

"But it *does* work," Speer Newman assured the crowd. "Right, Roy?"

Then came the welding stands, anvil, tongs, hardy, swage block, drifts of various sizes. Detached from a torch or forge, the metal-working gear looked colder than anything else in the hay yard. But Speer Newman got pretty good prices for all of it. So by the halfway point of the third row, he had more than proved himself, fighting off laryngitis, keeping up a friendly patter with the crowd, milking dollars out of stuff that even on a warm day would have been hard to sell. Not to mention dealing with Eileen, who was still peeved about the moving of the washtub. Roy felt for the guy.

In fact, his sympathy almost nullified *his* one and only com-plaint, which was too silly to bother Eileen with, almost too silly to admit to himself. "Now, folks," Speer Newman had said at the outset, "the Sebrights wanted me to convey their appreciation for your support today." It was auctioneer script. Roy knew that. But—*support*? Support was for 4-H sandwiches. Support was for walkathon disease research. Support was for abused pets and third-world orphans in hard-luck appeals on TV. He was only fifty-nine. It was embarrassing to have to hear such talk standing on property his father had homesteaded. For just a modest bid on each item displayed in this hay yard today, you can help provide this dear old couple with their daily ration of porridge and fiber pills! Varnished pity was what it was. And thirty-eight years of work and life ought to merit more than that.

There had been one compensation, though: the look on Cowboy Joe Leland's face when he figured out who old Rufus-Rafe-Roscoe was.

Autumn

"Go see for yourself: He looks all moony every time she bids, and she's been bidding a *lot*."

Eileen Sebright

By three o'clock, the day had long since seen its high temperature. The wind wasn't fierce, but it was now constant, and cold. Thickening clouds gave to the winter afternoon the look of premature dusk. The volume on the portable microphone was fading. And she was still being watched. At first she hadn't believed he was a banker; even on a warm day, a junior loan officer, especially one with a name like Cowboy Joe, wouldn't dress like that for an auction. "I'm telling you, Eileen," Roy had said, "that's the whole point about this guy."

What was he here for anyway—to make sure they didn't take the money and run? The thought was disturbingly pleasurable. She remembered the scandal a few years back, when that high-roller boat and snowmobile dealer over in Garland—and a member of the stake high council—cleaned out his till, bundled his snooty wife into a car due for repossession, and fled by night to Corpus Christi, Texas.

No, this Cowboy Joe Leland was not here to monitor receipts. Since noon, except when he went for a sandwich, he had stayed glued to the wall of the calving shed, all by himself, yet craving attention with his brown and gold. For all those years she would have liked to turn the tables on bankers—roam across *their* property, scrutinize *their* holdings, critique *their* methods—this one evoked only pity in her.

Even the microphone's static was fading. "We've saved the best of the small stuff for last," Speer Newman announced, pointing to a hand-crank corn sheller and a butter churn. "You don't find collectibles like this every day."

Eileen didn't care about the churn. Yet when it brought only seven dollars and fifty cents, she couldn't resist disappointment and foreboding. After the churn, the sheller brought an even five; the washboard, two-fifty. Several pairs of scissor-like wool shears, two kerosene lanterns, a brass porringer, a kneading trough whittled from pine heartwood, a trug, a trivet, a very old Dutch oven—Speer Newman practically had to give it all away. And now, just before the last table, there were six milk cans. One at a time or as a lot? Everybody, including Eileen, was praying for the latter. Please, please, please. People were cold and ready to get to the machinery or head home. A mailman from Cowley, a prim little fellow with round, wire-rimmed glasses, had the winning bid at three dollars each. Thank heavens he wanted all of them, told somebody his hobby was the making of novel ashtrays.

Trudy Pruitt

Just before the last table in the third row, the last table of all, the auctioneer pulled his hands out of too-thin gloves, blew on his fingers, and sneaked another look at her. Ordinarily Trudy Pruitt didn't put much stock in anything Dot Hennis said. Besides her eccentricities of dress, she was a gossip. But what if she was right?

What if he really was interested? Of *course* the kid working for him would say he was a nice guy, but Dot really *knew* because she knew of and about every auctioneer in the intermountain West. "Speer Newman is a keeper," she said.

At least he had shaved recently, wasn't wearing camouflage or leaking tobacco juice between stained lips. And he had to be better than that bozo in the brown and gold running suit. *Do you have a thing for tubs?* Thank goodness he didn't say *hot* tubs. He looked like the type who considered innuendo high-caliber flirting.

Yet ironically, the guy's perception was partly accurate. When she first saw it, the washtub evoked a pang of recognition and memory so strong as to almost distract her from Mr. Feinstein's crosscut saw. The summer Trudy Pruitt turned eleven, her grandparents celebrated their fiftieth anniversary with a reunion of their nine children and dozens of grandchildren. Two days her family traveled in a car, from Barstow to her grandparents' farm in Sutherlin, Oregon, just to meet and be with relatives.

At the center of the reunion memory was her grandfather's enormous washtub. It rested at the end of a long line of folding tables set up in the shade of an orchard, all of them draped with bedsheet tablecloths, bearing foil-covered bowls and platters and crock-pots and trays and trenchers. Fried chicken and potato salad and pie and ice cream to feed the five thousand. Fixed now on the tub wedged between saw and scythe, the eyes of thirty-seven-year-old Trudy Pruitt were again the eyes of her younger self, staring in awe as a wheelbarrow full of crushed ice obliterated the tub's ribbed bottom. Everything entrusted to that ice—every bottle of root beer and Orange Crush, every plum and peach—was made forever cold and sweet and delicious.

After the meal, they played kickball in an orchard clearing burnished by the setting sun. As darkness settled, there was a bonfire and much unhurried conversation and, in the fire's flickering shadows, a game of kick-the-can. In contrast to the sizzling pavements of Barstow, the orchard grass was as cool and lush as Eden, wonderfully hospitable to barefooted sprints.

She had wanted her children to know all that.

For the last time, Trudy, the answer is no.

III.

April

So, for the last of the collectibles, the very end of that third row, they swapped jobs: Autumn now sat up at the registration and payments table, and April stood beside her dad as clerk. The first thing noticeable from the clerk's vantage point was Cowboy Joe's subtle five-yard movement, from leaning against the wall of the calving shed to joining the little crowd of bidders. April had heard of Cowboy Joe Leland and had seen his reputation borne out this very day. An hour or so earlier, after buying his sandwich at the 4-H table, he had stepped over to hers and, while chewing barbecue meat and bun, had said, "Got a thing for tongue depressors?"

Lines of that kind explained why April Newman concentrated more on her dad's dating prospects than on her own. (At least Harley never tried to flirt; they were workmates, and that was it.) In the years since her mother's death, she had often wondered when his remorse would heal enough for him to reckon with his loneliness. If her sister was right, maybe today.

As it turned out, the bidding at the last table confirmed everything Autumn had said. As their dad chanted his auctioneer's chant, his gaze swept the crowd, as always, but lingered, with every pass, at Trudy Pruitt—a lingering even more pronounced now that the crowd had dwindled. And if Trudy Pruitt somehow didn't notice the extra attention during the selling of the scythe and hames, she could not have missed it when hers was the winning bid on the two-man crosscut saw. "Sold," he said, with a tone at once reflective and resolute, "to number fourteen."

Every Person Around the Plywood Table

The question now, in April Newman's mind, was whether that reflective resolution would motivate any action. The answer, of course, lay with the washtub. But April Newman couldn't know that yet. Nor could she know that the washtub was also the answer, or at least the catalyst, to the memory and desire and longing of every other person now gathered around the last table in the hay yard of this farm outside Balford, Wyoming.

One last small item to sell and two good reasons—a five-acre pasture full of unsold machinery and a sky threatening to refute her dad's weather forecast—to sell it quickly, and yet it was as if time hung fire. There the tub sat, between Speer Newman at one end of the plywood table and Trudy Pruitt at the other. There the tub sat, between Harley and the Sebrights, on one side, and, on the other, April, Dot Hennis, and Cowboy Joe. There it sat, the pot of the poker game. Every glance bounced off it, every stare was checked by it.

Auctioneer and junior loan officer both split their attention between the buyer in the purple ear warmer and the farmer's wife. The second buyer, hitching up her yellow long-johns and stamping her big laceless boots, split *her* attention between the auctioneer and her colleague, and tried, against stiff resistance—by means of nods and blinks, tics and twitches—to encourage one to at least acknowledge the interest of the other. For her part, the woman in the purple ear warmer kept looking at the auctioneer's daughter and admiring her name. The farmer's wife, discomfited by the scrutiny of the junior loan officer she had pitied, looked to her husband, who was returning that scrutiny measure for measure. And, finally, the daughter and apprentice, both soon to be surprised beyond their wildest imaginings, studied the man who would do the surprising. Oh so much working of human eyes around a table!

Shrewd. Wistful. Apologetic.

Conciliatory. Hopeful. Imploring.

What it held now, this old and empty washtub, far outweighed warble repellent or even bath water.

A curious expression came over Speer Newman's face.

"Folks," he announced, as time resumed, "if I'm going to have anything left for the machinery on the other side of the fence, I've got to give this voice of mine a rest."

Except for the lapse earlier in the day, his voice had been working just fine, better, in fact—as everyone knew—since the portable microphone had died. "Harley," he said, turning to his apprentice with utter decisiveness, "it's all yours."

"Now?" Harley asked, incredulous.

"Now would be just right," Speer Newman said, yielding his spot at the head of the plywood table. "You know what to do."

On one of Harley's last days at The Auctioneering School of America, Captain Duke had said that every new auctioneer must face his moment of truth. And this, Harley realized, was his. This was the moment he progressed beyond tomato cages. "Okay," he said. "O-*kay*! What do I hear? What'll you gonna give?" Nervously, he stroked his fuzzy mustache. Panache at three degrees above zero was no small challenge. "Come on, folks, who'll start? Five. Five. Five." He settled his ten-gallon hat on ears ruddy from the cold, blew into his clasped hands, then rubbed them together vigorously. "Who'll give me five? Five-five-five?"

If people were surprised when the first bid came from Cowboy Joe Leland, they were astonished when the second one came from Speer Newman. It was rare, perhaps even a breach of protocol, for an auctioneer to suddenly assume the role of buyer. His daughter could only stare in bewilderment and ask, "Do you need a number?"

He shook his head, kept his eye on the washtub and on Leland. "I think you can keep track of me."

Ten and then fifteen. Twenty. Twenty-five and thirty. The bids were prompt, willing, vigorous. Momentum was building. Harley, too, was wide-eyed and warming to his task. He turned ever so slightly toward April, the better to show off his fast-blooming prowess. This was what auctioneering was supposed to be. Suspense. Drama. The nuance of body language. Just as Captain Duke had taught. Like everybody else, though, Harley hoped that maybe body language—or something—would explain why either bidder *wanted* this washtub. Their answers would not have been simple. Each had a motive related to the woman in the ear warmer, and each had one related to the woman in the scarf. And in each, those motives collided.

Forty dollars. Forty-five. Speer held the bid, glanced at Trudy Pruitt.

Fifty-five. Then sixty. Cowboy Joe held the bid, glanced at Eileen Sebright.

The two women glanced at each other. That the bidding was a gesture of chivalry was a pretty safe conjecture, but chivalry from which man toward which woman, and to what end? What could either man know about either woman's interest in the old washtub? Or was the tub even relevant to what was going on? And all these questions were complicated by the undeniable rush from an unaccountable flattery.

Seventy. Seventy-five. Eighty. Bid and counterbid. Back and forth Harley swiveled his head, as if refereeing a Ping-Pong match. Up and up the price went. The auction had not seen this level of competitive tension all day. Back and forth. Up and up.

If pressed at this point, Trudy Pruitt would have guessed, without vanity, that both men were wooing her. And she would have concluded, with some disappointment, that Cowboy Joe Leland's brashness in flirting was duplicated in his bidding, and that that brashness, of all things, would win the tub. Eileen Sebright's guess would have had both men ingratiating themselves to her, though the auctioneer's much clearer need for such would have forced her, with some disappointment, to predict Speer Newman's triumph.

Both women would have been as wrong as they were right.

A hundred and ten. Now twenty. Now thirty-five. Bid after bid, increment after increment, neither man hesitated. Until they approached the plateau of one hundred and fifty dollars.

"Now fifty," Harley chanted, "one-fifty, fifty, fifty!"

It was Speer's turn to bid, but this time he didn't. He looked at Eileen Sebright and the washtub, and then at Trudy Pruitt. And the *way* he looked at them made it clear just what they had been wrong about. He wasn't stopping because of timidity or a shallow pocket. A hundred and fifty dollars was a lot of money for a washtub he wasn't really interested in. And at that moment it occurred to him—and them, too—that what he *was* interested in couldn't be had for bidding anyway.

"Will you give me fifty?" Harley cried, looking at his boss, inviting the next bid with tilted head, raised eyebrows, and a slightly theatrical upturning of his palm. "Come on, fifty?"

On his side of the table, Leland was suddenly, sickeningly aware that his pride's reach had exceeded his wallet's grasp about a hundred and twenty dollars back. Now that he had the bid, he didn't want it. If he wasn't outbid, he would have to default. He looked at Trudy Pruitt and at the washtub, and then at Eileen Sebright. The most troubling consequence of defaulting was not, as he might earlier have supposed, the prospect of a Monday morning reprimand (or worse) from his boss; the most troubling consequence was failing in his quest to return the tub to its owner—which Eileen realized the very same instant she realized his predicament.

"A hunnerd forty-five going twice . . ."

The two bidders looked at each other.

A heavy pause, as before the squeeze of the trigger, the fall of the blade, the last millimeter of fuse. Just as Harley's tonsils and tongue and teeth were conspiring to say what had to be said, just at that moment, the cold air was rent with the loud, manly bray of the yellow-legged Dot Hennis. "One-fifty it is!" she hollered.

EPILOGUE

Just after the tub sold, the wind let up, and some who had planned to leave at that point in the auction, during the ten-minute break before the field machinery, didn't. Others, still wary of the sky, hurried to load their newly purchased goods and be gone.

Roy Sebright lingered among the aisles to help with the loading and to watch people carry away the goods accumulated in a working life. Just a few months earlier he had helped with the last loading of his cattle. Only someone acquainted with selling out could know how suddenly household and farmyard spaces are emptied.

"Caught up in the excitement of bidding, Mr. Sebright," said the mailman from Cowley, "I was not mindful of the cargo capacity of a Volkswagen Beetle." The lenses of his wire-rimmed glasses had fogged over. "Would you mind too much if I left my milk cans with you until tomorrow, when I can come back with my brother's pickup truck?"

Roy was only too happy to oblige, to forestall the emptying even in a small way. He unwired the latch of the door to the calving shed and helped carry the cans out of the weather. He lined them up against the long wall, next to the only other objects to be seen—a pitchfork missing a tine and a water hose with no couplings.

"No hurry," Roy told the mailman. "They'll be right here."

When they stepped out of the shed, the first snowflakes were floating downward. In the windless calm, the only force acting on them was gravity.

Meanwhile, with the ten-minute break now spent, bidders on the other side of the sucker-rod fence had congregated around a three-bottom plow whose shares and moldboards were worn thin. They looked to Harley for their cues. Though April hadn't come with him as clerk, she had appointed a substitute—a high school senior from the 4-H refreshment table.

"Just while her and her dad take a little break," the 4-H girl said.

"No hurry," Harley assured her.

The brim of his hat was catching an impressive quantity of snowflakes.

In front of the refreshment table, the basketball game long forgotten, Cowboy Joe Leland handed Mrs. Sebright a cup of hot chocolate, a gesture of consolation for them both. She blew on the steaming liquid, took a sip, then said, "I wouldn't have had room for it anyway."

She was referring, of course, to the washtub, which now rested on the ground only twenty feet away, just inches behind the laceless boots of its new owner. "Trudy Pruitt, don't you even think of taking off in this weather," Dot Hennis said. "Get yourself a room right here in Balford. Start for home tomorrow, maybe even Monday."

Trudy was only half-listening. She kept staring at the washtub, at the way the rim circumscribed and swallowed the falling snowflakes. In her heart, she had already been persuaded.

"There's more goes on weekends in a place like this than you might think," Dot said.

Not very far away, Speer Newman submitted to some coaching of his own. Maybe, Autumn suggested, Ms. Trudy Pruitt could use a hand loading the things she had bought, especially that crosscut saw. And maybe, April added, she would like to come to dinner with them.

When he nodded without moving, each daughter placed one hand at the small of his back and, through the layers of coat and coveralls, nudged him in the direction he needed to go.

SKY-LOFT LOVELIES

LAST THING VIRLINGER WANTED TO KNOW WAS DID I *comprender* girls. Five weeks training the guy, and that's his good-bye? He's standing there in front of the Salado pension and goes, "What I mean, Elder Haymore, is she's my *cousin*." What's he think—I'm so hick I'm going to sling this Sue Darlington over my shoulder the minute I get home? He's the one brought her up, the night before, when he's digging that splinter out of my calf. We're just walking along, my last night in Ecuador, and I end up between him on the ground and that jerk *taxista* yelling at him where to stick his Mormon pamphlet. When I said that's enough, I thought the guy was going to punch me. With sunset and the weeds, I couldn't see the drop-off where I was stepping in all that broken bamboo matting. Back at the pension, you should've seen Virlinger's eyes when he asked for a pin or something sharp and I pull that commando knife out of my duffel. That's when he goes, "I got somebody you need to look up when you get home." He made me promise.

So—what? He sleeps on it and next morning decides maybe this match-up is a long shot. He waits until me and the duffel are loaded in one of those Toyota *camionetas* thirty years old, headed to the mission home for the group meal and van to the airport, and *then* he wonders do I know anything about girls?

No. I already told him that. If you want somebody can *comprender* girls, ask Ogleby or Riggs; they got girlfriends waiting. Ask Clair Elroy. He doesn't, but he'll make something up. But me, I got zero experience. Except for that little stretch at BYU, fall semester '83, all I did in my life was hunt and build cabins with my dad and Uncle Dewart—Haymore Scenic Homes. Before I know it, I'm twenty-five, walking in the Missionary Training Center, and never been out with a girl. It's weird, I know. That's mostly the reason I decided, right at the cut-off, to go ahead and go. Two years doing what a missionary does couldn't *hurt* my chances. That's basically what President Arnold said in my last interview, before the farewell meal, urging me to get on with life. I agree. I don't want to end up like my Uncle Hewell over in Wyoming—thirty-three years old and no wife yet, still living with Grandma Edrus. That's what I kept reminding myself on the red-eye from Guayaquil to Miami.

What I didn't tell Virlinger about was Dishroom. That's where I worked that half semester at college. If you want to *comprender* girls, Food Services during lunch shift is a good place to start. They're even color-coded. White dresses in Vegetable Prep, Pastry, and Dishroom. Orange dresses back in Salads, Ethnic, Entree—and all the serving lines out front. They all complained about how the material looked like canvas and what the hairnets did to their hair. Dishroom girls had it even worse. You could always tell them from their melted makeup. Anywhere close to the dishwasher—the thing's long as a combine—it's like you're working in a sauna or carwash. About that noisy, too.

Except for sisters and cousins, Dishroom's the only place I've ever really had anything to do with girls. Church and school didn't count for much; girls there kind of went around me like a wormy log, probably like they do Uncle Hewell. So it was a new deal for me to be where they were for any stretch of time, like that first day I worked with these two named Kyung-hee and Chaz.

"So we got Korea and Walla Walla and now Mink Creek, Idaho." That's what Chaz said when I met them. "The world is well represented."

During noon rush, the three of us stood side by side at one of the prep belts feeding the dishwasher. There was another prep belt and two girls on that one, too—and Gord the student supervisor. And between the belts was the drain trough for all the ice and drink left in glasses. During rush, it took every one of us to handle the loaded trays coming in from the dining room. Tall glasses, short glasses, plates, bowls, silverware. It all kept coming and coming like it'd never stop.

But nothing rattled Chaz. Not sloshing in an inch of water from the leaky drain trough and leaky spray hoses hanging by leaky soaker sinks on the wall behind us. Not trash bags rupturing. Not trays clattering from a pile-up, plates and glasses shattering all over the floor. And the only thing in my life came anywhere close to the smell of those trash cans was trying to go too fast skinning and accidentally nicking the paunch.

She was always cheerful, wore her name button like a headlamp, hooked to her hairnet with all these bobby pins. She's the one girl in my life ever actually said more to me than, "Hi, I've got a boyfriend on a mission." And there was one time it was more than talk. That's what I'm thinking of. It's nothing much, but if I'd thought to tell Virlinger, maybe he wouldn't sweat giving me his cousin's name. He's got enough worries with his bad eyes and stomach bugs.

The thing is, with the hairnets and aprons, Dishroom girls sometimes didn't even *look* female. Except working next to Chaz, I was always really aware she was. It's odd to say, but I liked her elbows. I used to watch her and Kyung-hee for reasons you don't usually watch girls. I'm okay fast with a hammer or hatchet, but there was no keeping up with them. When the rush was heaviest, they didn't even bother with a spatula. One swipe with a green rubber glove, and bones and gravy and crusts and sauce and napkins just disappeared into the trash can. Even with Gord helping, the girls on the other prep belt had pile-ups all the time, way more than Chaz and Kyung-hee.

Tending the belts was just part of it. There was *always* something crusty waiting by the soaker sinks, and Dishroom got pegged to clean everybody's mess in the whole place. It's like we were everybody's janitor. Broken glass somewhere, we swept; any kind of spill, we mopped. A hundred other people can *see* the trash compactor needs emptying or is jammed and leaking nasty juice, but they just keep dropping junk in it, waiting for somebody from Dishroom. And weird dirty jobs, too. One time I had to hose fifteen tubs of half-melted ice cream down the disposal. You think, ice cream, yum. But not this stuff—not all that foamy butter pecan and rocky road swirling around a half-clogged drain. Looking long enough at a sinkful of something like that, it's hard not to think of every bad flush in your whole life. It made me half queasy.

On my first day, the manager they'd just hired didn't make this pecking order clear at all. His name was Doyle Dunn. The only thing he said to me was Dishroom guys had to wear the paper hat but not the orange bow tie, on account of the rubber apron. Then he told me to find Gord. He said, "You look like a horse who's not afraid of a little heavy pulling." He said, "You'll get along fine." My orientation took him all of thirty seconds, and he never got anywhere close to the dishwasher, let alone the prep belts or soaker sinks. He didn't want to get his Hush Puppies wet. Every day after that, when he bothered to step foot in the place at all, he'd stop at the silverware burnisher up front and do his managing from there, mostly clipping his fingernails and playing with his necktie. He was always chewing gum, too, which is a big no-no in Food Services

It wasn't the work I minded. Digging footers in rocky ground is harder by a mile, and going up to people on the mission takes more guts. In the job office, the only thing left after Dishroom was midnight janitor in one of the gym locker rooms, and I would've taken it. Compared to what I saw in Ecuador, scrubbing toilets and urinals would've been a treat. Their idea of a public bathroom down there is thirty guys behind a flimsy bus station wall peeing in a long tin trough. So I'm not talking picky. But the pecking order? I don't like gofering. Even when people are nice about asking, it gets old fast.

Orange and white wasn't all there was in Food Services. There was this place upstairs called Sky Loft. Up there they eat off the college's nice plates. So you dig through your mashed potatoes or whatever, and you got the BYU logo staring you in the face. Chaz is the one who told me Sky Loft had waiters and hostesses; she pointed them out to me. They clock in down where everybody else does, by the main water fountain, but up there's a whole different world. The guys wear normal black ties and Sunday pants and shoes. And those girls—they were something.

Chaz called them lovelies, had to explain the word to Kyung-hee. She wasn't being mean, but you'd have to be blind not to notice they got a lot more attention than orange and white. And Chaz wasn't blind. She asked did I know why a brand new Dishroom manager was never in the dishroom. Because he's a deadbeat doesn't want to get his shoes wet, right? She said yeah, definitely that, but he could deadbeat anywhere, so why keep moseying up to Sky Loft? She said obviously because he likes the view. Maybe it was the nice dresses of their own and the high heels—and no hairnet. The lovelies even got their own special Sky Loft name tag and not just a pin-on button in Magic Marker. Chaz goes, "Let us come to work gussied up, and we wouldn't be half bad ourselves." She sort of looks at Kyung-hee to back her up. "Myron here doesn't even know what we look like off-duty, does he?" Uncle Dewart would say I was some kind of dense to miss a hint like that.

Noon shift every day, out in the back hall by the mop room and racks of buns, the lovelies open a closet-looking door to this spiral metal staircase, steps coiled so tight around a center pole it feels almost like you're in a silo. "There they go, up to the highest degree of glory." Chaz was joking about that. She said most the ones she'd known in her three semesters were pretty nice; just once in a while, one of them would start believing the higher-glory thing, especially with Dishroom. Especially with Dishroom *guys*. She said last winter semester Gord got a killer crush on a lovely named Natalie. Natalie let on like she was sort of interested too, but what she was really interested in was impressing one of the black-ties. So she sweet-talked Gord into doing all the grunt chores black-ties were supposed to do when things were slow—bricking their grill, carting trash, hauling ice from somewhere else when Sky Loft's machine was on the blink. Which was always.

According to Chaz, none of that was Dishroom's job. Anybody didn't believe her could check the official list of duties tacked on the bulletin board, along with the choking diagram and all the wedding announcements. The only thing we were supposed to do for Sky Loft was wash the dishes they brought down to us. Then Chaz got a little bossy, like she sometimes did, and told me to watch out for the lovelies. But I didn't see the problem. When was I ever going to get up to Sky Loft? Chaz goes, "That's what Gord said."

For three weeks that's all I did was help wash their dirty dishes. Every day, about the time our rush is slacking off, we hear the cargo elevator, and here comes two or three black ties and their big steel cart. They're supposed to roll it all the way back to the soaker sinks, not just ditch it by the burnisher. I couldn't blame them for wanting dry feet, but those weenies wouldn't even say thanks, not even "Hi" or "How you doing?" One time, just when they're tip-toeing out, Chaz hollers, "You're *welcome!*" Of course, with the racket, they acted like they didn't hear her.

Then one day I'm at one of the sinks with a wad of steel wool, working on a colander somebody in Pastry used for this fruit syrup crap with a zillion seeds, dried on like stucco. We're waiting for the cart. Pretty quick Chaz tugs at my apron, and she's pointing. There's Doyle Dunn, with his Hush Puppies on dry ground, waving for me to come on. He could see for himself, but he goes, "Say, Myron, you busy?" He takes me out by the racks of buns and porta-warmers, and, boom, standing right there there's this girl from Sky Loft. Her name tag says *Head Hostess Markie.* Her dress is pretty close to BYU modest, but if there's ever a female deserved Chaz's label, it was this one. Hair, face, body—she was unbelievable. Doyle Dunn's fifty years old and going bald, but he's sucking in his gut big-time. Markie's perfume had that effect. Real friendly, he tells me Sky Loft's extra busy catering a sports banquet in some back room upstairs and doesn't have a hand to spare. Then he tells Markie I'll be glad to help her out, goes, "This guy's a horse."

"Thank you *so* much." She's totally fake and not even looking at me when she says it, but it's like, dang, she's pretty. So there's me and Doyle following the high heels and legs all the way up the spiral staircase, trying to keep our eyes and minds where they belong. We come out on this hallway, and right there's the big cart stacked with dirty BYU dishes. From the hallway, I'm looking straight into the Sky Loft dining room, people eating at tables with table cloths, everything windows and mountains in the sunshine. The strange thing is there's black ties and high heels all over the place, standing around laughing and joking—plenty of hands to spare. Doyle goes, "So can we get that cart downstairs for her, Myron?" He said *we,* but he disappeared almost faster than Markie.

When I got back with the cart, the dishroom was quiet for a change. Gord's kneeling by the combine, like he did every day after rush, pulling out the debris screens. How to get them in and out is secret student supervisor stuff. The only thing he'd let me do is bang them over a trash can to get all the coleslaw-looking crud out of them and hose them clean. So when I go to bang and hose this time, he's looking at me real funny, and he's not the only one. Right after Gord uses his other supervisor powers to flip the switch on the dishwasher, Chaz leaves Kyung-hee swiping pork chop bones off the BYU plates and comes right up to me, nice elbows and all, and says, "Don't tell me lovely Markie conned you into shagging their dirty dishes." I said of course not; it was Doyle Dunn had me bring them down. But Chaz didn't believe me. She could smell the perfume. Anything in that place *doesn't* smell like paunch gas and steel wool, you're going to notice. She goes, "That's a job for all her boyfriends up there, and Doyle knows it."

I knew it, too. The thing is, I didn't exactly mind. There's always this little idiot corner in the back of your brain says maybe something you do matters to a girl like Markie, even when she keeps proving you wrong. Like the next time, she didn't even bother coming down to the main floor herself. She just sent Doyle Dunn. If it was any of those black-tie weenies asking, I would've said take a hike. But if Markie wanted something—ice or trash or bricking the grill—even if I had to hear it from Doyle, away I went, lickety-split. All the time I was hoping to run into her, maybe get sweet-talked myself, fake or not, or at least smell her. But she never came my way, never left her head-hostess podium except to walk here and there in her high heels to say friendly stuff to Sky Loft people.

About the third time I came down with the cart, Chaz steps up to me—she was shorter by quite a bit—and touches my shoulder with a rubber spatula. She's clowning like she's casting a spell. "You are hereby rescued from the clutches of all Sky Loft lovelies." But she's not joking so much when she says the black ties know their way to the dishroom and dumpster just as good as I do. Then she puts her *hand* on my shoulder. Even through the glove, I can feel her fingers. I'm looking at her headlamp name button and her face shiny from steam and her eyes really clear and pretty, and I'm thinking *this* is the girl worth shagging dirty dishes for.

The spell worked a little. A few days later, here comes Doyle Dunn. "Say, Myron, you busy?" He says Sky Loft's straining fryer oil and is out of filters. Can I hustle some up to them before they start on egg rolls to go with their stir-fry special? We're just starting into rush, so what I really wonder is why he can't hustle some up himself. I said I hated to leave Chaz and Kyung-hee shorthanded. Doyle says they're Dishroom pros, they'll survive without me for a few minutes. So I come right out and ask was it Markie wanting the filters or the guy actually cooking the egg-rolls? For just a second, Doyle Dunn's gum chewing slows way down, and he looks busted. And then he looks sort of ticked. "Why don't you let me worry about who's asking what, Myron."

I should've figured it'd be more than filters. You don't need a horse for that. Doyle didn't say anything about somebody straining the oil too hot and melting right through the wall of the plastic catch-bucket. The slick ran all over Sky Loft's kitchen floor. I spent the rest of my shift with a broken-handled squeegee and a mop.

When I got back to the punch-clock, almost a half hour overtime, Chaz was waiting. She had changed into normal clothes and combed her hair way puffier than the hairnet would ever let it be. For a minute she's just looking at me. Then, like she's been thinking it over, she goes, "Next to Kyung-hee, you are my best dishroom bud, Myron Haymore. I need you down here." She's got her hand on my arm when she's saying all this. "If Doyle won't do anything about it, I'll go to Markie or whoever I have to go to." I told her I'd make it up to Kyung-hee for hosing out my trash cans. Chaz said that wasn't what she meant. She comes right out and says she's tired of Markie playing Dishroom for a bunch of dupes. But who she means is me.

For the first time I could see wrists and hands. I really liked Chaz. From nineteen on, I always got asked was I going on a mission pretty soon or had I been on one, like that was my ticket to being okay. But not with Chaz. Right then, after Sky Loft's oil mess, if I'd invited her to go get something to eat on one of the plates we washed every day, or somewhere off campus, or maybe go see a movie that night, she would've gone. I know she would've. On a lot of long streets in Ecuador, a lot of nights staring through a mosquito net, I wondered how I could've been so coward or moron not to ask *something*.

Chaz talked to Doyle Dunn and Markie both. Doyle was at least polite about telling her to mind her own business. Markie said if she and Kyung-hee were tired of Dishroom, they could put their names on the Sky Loft waiting list, but not to get their hopes up. After Chaz told her what she could do with her waiting list, I couldn't even fool myself that I'd been gofering for Sky Loft just so this girl with really nice elbows wouldn't have to. Because Chaz never would've stood for it in the first place.

All through that half semester at BYU, what I really didn't *comprender* was me. The Saturday after the fryer oil, I saw Markie at a football game. Me and a roommate were two rows behind her and her date and this other couple. She didn't much like the guy she was with—you could tell—and kept trying to flirt with the other one. But the other guy seemed happy enough with his own date, and Markie's football-game clothes and really pretty face and done-up hair and even that body of hers didn't seem to matter. It's odd, but I felt bad for her. One time, when everybody stands up for the fight song, she turns around, scoping the crowd, and looks right at me. But without my apron and goofy-looking paper hat, she didn't have a clue who I was. But what's even weirder is this: If she'd asked me, right then, to fetch hotdogs and popcorn for the double date that wasn't going so good, I probably would've done it.

But that did finally change my last day in Dishroom. Just before rush, I'm up on a step-ladder cleaning the grease hood over the ovens in the downstairs kitchen, and it's Gord tugging on my apron this time, asking where I've been hiding. He says they got an emergency up in Sky Loft, and Chaz and Kyung-hee are already on the elevator with a mop bucket and rags. So where's Doyle is the natural question, and Gord goes, "AWOL on this one; you'll see why."

By that time in the semester, I'd done some pretty nasty clean-ups. But nobody throwing up yet. When Gord told me that, I came down off the ladder. He starts explaining about shutting down our belt and somebody having to stay and tend the other one, so he's *entrusting* me with the Sky Loft situation—big smile on his face—because I know my way around up there so well. There was no need for the snow job; I was already headed to the mop room. This was my mess way more than it was Kyung-hee's or Chaz's.

Gord told me a whisk broom works about as good as any-thing for a first pass on carpet, *if* you go heavy with the sawdust. So that's what I got, a whole big ketchup can full of cedar sawdust, that and the whisk broom and metal dustpan, and I took those spiral steps two at a time. It felt weird busting out the door at the top of the staircase and going straight on into the dining room, completely ignoring the dish cart in the Sky Loft hallway, like everybody else does. Chaz was just wheeling the mop bucket off the elevator, and Kyung-hee was carrying a normal bucket full of this anti-bacterial cleanser mix. Chaz is all smiles when she sees me, and she goes, "Three semesters here, and *this* is what it takes for me to get up to the highest degree of glory?"

Somebody throwing up in a place like that pretty much kills the lunch business, so naturally the Sky Loft manager's antsy. This one was a lady, a *big* lady; I'd never seen her before. I never did know her name. When she sees us coming, her cheeks light up, and she says, "You three are an answer to a prayer." Then she can finally turn to the crowd and say, "We'll have this cleaned up right away, folks." Because of her size and the big dress covering it and shoes about as ladylike as combat boots, people believed her. She was real nice, even when she was asking where Doyle was, didn't want to sound like she was blaming us for not knowing.

There was no yellow tape or anything, but you didn't need it. Just like in grade school—it never changes—faces waiting for the clean-up crew are all looking for the exact *location*. It's like you sort of want to see it, and not just so you know where to steer clear of, but so you can get grossed out without having to do anything about it. Unless you're Dishroom.

It was bad. It looked like a whole stomachful in a trail from the buffet tile to the carpet where people walk in the place. Of course that's where the head hostess podium is, too, by the little sign says *Please Wait to Be Seated.* So while I'm sprinkling cedar sawdust, I'm wondering could it be Markie did the throwing up. But, no, I hear some guy talking to the stout manager lady, apologizing over and over about his wife being pregnant and feeling fine, and then this. And then I see Markie herself, standing off to the side with some other lovelies and a few black ties. She's not looking too happy, which makes you wonder—what's *she* got to be sore about? Nobody likes it, but you got to feel sort of bad for the person just blew lunch special all over the dining room floor, even if it did make a puddle by your hostess podium.

So there's Chaz mopping the far end of the buffet tile and me kneeling with the whisk broom and dustpan, breathing through my mouth, trying to funnel the first load back into the ketchup can. It doesn't take long to figure out not all the trail clean-up's going to fit. And I didn't bring anything else. But Kyung-hee's way ahead of me. She steps behind the podium and grabs this pretty little gold-colored wastebasket. That's when somebody yells, "Hey! What are you doing?" In two seconds Markie's high heels and ankles are almost under my nose, and she goes, "That's my wastebasket." Kyung-hee just smiles like she no speak-a English—even though she understands Markie crystal clear—and goes ahead and holds it for me. So now Markie's in *my* face, asking me, "Did *you* hear what I said?" Everybody in the whole place heard what she said. I told her I'd bleach it good afterward, and then went right ahead and dumped.

Markie was ticked. She starts in promising wherever Doyle Dunn is, he's going to hear about how I'm rude, how I just ruined her wastebasket, how I don't know my job. She's getting even louder, so the manager lady comes over, tells her to calm down. She says these things happen and Dishroom's doing the best they can to get everything back to normal. Markie didn't like hearing any of it, takes one more look at her wastebasket, then walks off in a huff. That's when Kyung-hee says something I really hope is juicy Korean for somebody who'd whine about a three-gallon wastebasket that never had any *real* trash in it anyway—just gum and mint wrappers, little stuff like that.

When Chaz finished mopping, she helped us rag-scrub the carpet with the bucket of anti-bacterial mix. Kyung-hee finished first and headed back downstairs to see if Gord wanted to open our belt back up for the rest of rush. People in Sky Loft were drifting off, nothing to look at now. The stout manager lady went around apologizing to everybody and inviting them to have some dessert on the house. Nothing like a nice fudge brownie with a scoop of vanilla ice cream on top to put the world right. That's what she said. Next time I looked up, she was gone. And right then, like she'd timed it that way, I swear, here comes Markie, with Doyle Dunn trying to keep up. His comb-over's hanging wrong, and he's holding an old can of air freshener I know for a fact is empty.

With our boss there now and her boss not, Markie's all of a sudden sitting pretty. First thing she does is look hard at the mopped buffet tile and tell Chaz to go find some *Wet Floor* signs.

She goes, "We don't need another incident today," like the throwing up was Chaz's fault. The way they were looking at each other, I thought Chaz was going to say something, and I would've liked to hear it. But Doyle just nods for her to go ahead for the signs.

Now that she's got Doyle there, looking for something to spray with his empty air freshener can, Markie turns to me. With the rag and anti-bacterial stuff, I was scrubbing the last of the carpet stains, quite a ways from the podium. "And do you see what *he* did to my wastebasket?" Doyle takes a look, but even he's wondering what's the big deal. He goes, "That's nothing a new liner won't fix, Markie. And we've got plenty of those." You should've seen her face. She goes, "I want that emptied and sterilized *immediately.*"

That's when she goes to white-gloving the hostess podium, top to bottom. She stops a long time at the base, then looks at me and says, "Who cleaned this?"

It was Chaz did the scrubbing on that end of the trail. But I wasn't about to tell Markie that. I wasn't much interested in whatever she had to say about dirty-work scrubbing she had no part in. So I said the podium looked clean enough to me.

Oh boy. I thought she was going to spit on me. She takes a deep breath, folds her arms in her super-bod Markie way, and says, "Maybe Sky Loft has a little higher standard than you're used to."

It's not something you're going to talk much about with somebody like Markie, but, you know, how far does something like that splatter? Two or three feet, tops? So the podium's out of range, and she's freaking for no reason. But Doyle's looking at me like what would it hurt to go one more lick with my rag, if it'd keep the lovely Markie happy—and keep the heat off him for coming late to the emergency.

I know it's no big thing I'm telling here. Chaz didn't need me to do what I did; whatever she would've said or not said to Markie, she would've been just fine on her own. See, I didn't know she was coming back down the hall and watching everything; I wouldn't have guessed she could get back with the *Wet Floor* signs so quick. So when I stood up to move the bucket of anti-bacterial cleanser closer to the podium, I was thinking this was just between me and Markie. Though I admit when I dunked my rag one last time in mix that's probably breeding a lot more bacteria than it's killing by now—and only half wrung it out—I did remember the rubber spatula on my shoulder.

Markie looks at me like this horse isn't moving fast enough to suit her, so she says, "I want it really *clean* this time, okay?"

I said okay, but instead of going to the podium, I took a step toward her. She looked at me sort of funny. Then she looked at me *real* funny when I asked her to hold out her hand for just a second. I mean, that's a hand that's never in her life done any chucking and swiping. But she actually did it. And before the surprise wore off, I filled that lovely hand with the dripping anti-bacterial rag and said, "Better scrub hard."

That's what I could've said for myself when Virlinger asked what he asked that last morning in front of the Salado pension. But I don't know, somebody who'd do what I did to Markie—you should've heard what came out of those pretty lips—might not be what he has in mind for his cousin Sue Darlington. But this was before Ecuador. After two years of getting told to eat *boñiga*, Yankee fag spy, and getting egged during *carnivál* and one time even catching a rock, I probably wouldn't even fool with answering Markie now. But back then what she did bugged me bad. Even if Doyle Dunn hadn't threatened to fire me from Dishroom—how was keeping Markie happy going to save *his* hide?—I probably still would've quit.

But quitting wasn't my biggest muff. It's Chaz I blew it with.

She liked me. After the rag thing, back in the hall by the cart of dirty dishes, she hugged me really tight, then kissed me. She honestly did. We could've gone out. There was no need to quit my classes and go play mountain man by myself in those can-yons behind Provo until the snow came hard—then beat it back to Mink Creek without saying hi or bye to *anybody*. Twenty-five, and no girl had ever been the least bit interested in me. Seems now like the stupidest thing I could've done, to walk away from one who was.

And that was it until almost the year mark in Ecuador, in this place called Ancón out on the peninsula, my third month with a companion named Orquiza. The guy hated Americans, especially dishroom workers from Mink Creek, Idaho. One mail day I get a wedding announcement postmarked Walla Walla. She knew where I was. *To my best dishroom bud.* That's what she wrote. During *siesta* on a really hot afternoon, I laid there on my cot and read that line a hundred times. In between I stared at Chaz's picture in the announcement. No hairnet. No name button. No rubber gloves. She was in a really nice dress, with her hand on the shoulder of this guy she's already married to by the time the announcement made it to South America. She hardly looked like the Chaz I remembered next to me on the dish belt, except for the eyes and the smile. And the elbows.

Even if I'd told all this to Virlinger, I doubt I could've explained how that picture made me feel. No need to ever bring that up with Sue Darlington—if we do end up meeting—but she is going to wonder how I got to be twenty-seven and just barely coming home from a mission. My only real hope is if she's anything like Chaz, she'll understand.

SPINSTERS AND THEIR DREAMS

YOU'RE LUCKY, OWEN. THAT BIG NURSE MURIEL IS A gem. A couple of those that empty bedpans roll their eyes every time they walk in on me, but not Muriel. She says to me, "Go ahead and talk to him, Ivy. They hear more than you think." What she doesn't know is old Ivy's talking for her own sake. And here in a little bit I'm not going to have your ears for such indulgence. Muriel says hospice is scheduled next week. Nice ladies, but after them, it's the knacker wagon. First Mother, then Dad, and now you—my own twin. I'm no whiner, and I don't begrudge you wanting to be with Nelda, but I am feeling a little forsaken. Here I make it to 2009, and I have nobody to celebrate with. Oh, your kids are good to me. I'm not saying that. You've got a lovely posterity. But they're not *you*.

But if it's my lot to be the last of our generation to go, you have my solemn promise: I will not let the obituary writer of the *Balford Clarion* refer to you as Owen "Jersey" Teague. It's a little late to confess, but I hate hearing you called that. If the men in this town thought you had to have a silly barber-shop nickname, there were better choices than a breed of cow, even if it was the one you stocked your dairy with for fifty years.

"What you got against Holsteins?" Big Frett Maxwell wanted to know. Do you remember? "Nothing," you said, "except Balford Creamery's willing to contract for thirteen cents more per hundred for something with a little more butterfat." Frugal as you were through four years in the Army and eight more in the oil fields down in Lamont, you already had a lot saved. With Big

Frett, money talks. I would've loved to see his face when you spread your plans for a parlor and holding tank across his big banker's desk.

I know, I know. Mother wasn't the *first* to go. And it's not dairy farming I came here to talk to you about. Until the other night, what happened to our little brother was all tucked away in the past. Then out of the blue, I had this dream with his head-stone in it.

LOOMIS ARLIN TEAGUE
NOV. 28, 1925–NOV. 28, 1941

By then, the very day he turned sixteen, Arlin hadn't let us sing to him in three or four years, said we sounded like a bunch of starved alley cats. But that didn't stop Mother from *threatening* to sing that last time. If you weren't so doped up these days, you could at least recognize the face of your old-maid sister and maybe tell her if *that* was why Arlin was so evasive about when you two might be back from your hunt? He just kept fiddling with the scope on his birthday rifle.

"Arlin, honey, I'm talking to you."

To go with her chocolate cake, she was planning to make ice cream. All she wanted to know was when to start it. The week before, just a couple of days after Thanksgiving, the weather had turned cold, but ice cream's what he wanted. And no complaint from me or you. Put us in a snow hut in Mongolia, and we'd ask for ice cream. Little did we know how long it would be before we saw any in that house again.

When I turned forty, Bishop Clive Sebright assured me it wasn't only men who dream dreams and see visions. He was the first farmer for a bishop we'd had in quite a while, from that whole family of Sebrights that farmed down by the Loop. He meant well. He was just saying what bishops have to say to the likes of me—the Lord cares about spinsters too, etcetera. Which

I never doubted. By then—that would've been 1964—I had my own house and flower garden, a good job clerking in the post office, two weeks' paid vacation every year. But, with due respect to Bishop Sebright, my visions and dreams have never amounted to much.

Until the other night. Most mornings I can't think of the paperboy's name, and now—from the dream or not, I can't say—I'm remembering *details* from almost seventy years ago. Like Arlin saying, "You can't come with us this time, Ivy. This is real hunting now, and it don't mix with talking." Since when was I unfit company on one of our outings? And *you* wouldn't have minded having me along, gabby or not. If I had gone, you wouldn't have had to bear so much alone. I can still see you showing back up at the house in that ratty stocking cap you used to wear, panting and dripping sweat, despite the cold. "Something's wrong," you said. You said when you got back from flushing the willow bars up the river, you found the new rifle propped against the trunk of a Russian olive, but no Arlin. Then you said the oddest thing: "You should see what a mess a .30/06 makes of a goose."

"Goose?" Mother asked. She turned to Dad and said, "You told me that rifle you gave him was for *deer*." Dad turned straight to you and said, "So you just went off and left him—when that's the very thing I told you *not* to do?"

Actually, I don't think Dad had said either thing. He and Mother were both sick with dread, and dread does strange things to thoughts and words.

Imagine. Their only "natural" child, as people used to say, and he's the one they lose. Why shouldn't they have felt something special for him? He was a wonder and a refutation both. During their engagement, a doctor had told Mother, "Young lady, a brick has more chance of conceiving." I know Mother could be pretty quick to conjure rude intent out of nothing more malicious than clumsiness. But such news certainly could've been more gently put to a bride-to-be, especially since the premarital examination—"down there"—had probably already mortified her. She was what—eighteen?

Even if I had stayed behind with Mother when you two went back down to the river bluffs to find Arlin, I would've been no comfort to her. And I didn't want to hear *again* how Arlin needed to socialize more with kids from church and school, spend less time traipsing through riverbottom pasture hoping to shoot something. When I went out the back door, she was sitting at the kitchen table, turning and turning the crank on a bucket of ice cream that would never get eaten. It was eerie how she stared out the window, holding that handle as if life depended on it. It took a mile trotting through sagebrush and alkali to catch up with you and Dad, and another mile crunching through frozen swamp for us to get to the beaver pond. Even with the light fading fast, we right away spotted the mess of bloody feathers out toward the middle of the ice.

That was Arlin's doing, no doubt about it. It wasn't cruelty or destructiveness behind such things, but more like a curiosity, a dare all his own, with no regard whatsoever for a consequence. I can still see him in the stubble of the hay field, when he was twelve or thirteen, jabbing a pitchfork at that rattlesnake. Strike, jab, strike, jab. You told him not to be a fool, to quit messing and kill it outright. He paid no attention. Only when he tired of the game did he finally whack the snake with the back of the tines, to stun it enough so he could stab it right between the eyes. Then he hoisted the fork high, held all three feet in the air, and said, "*Now* who's the fool?"

Now listen, I don't want to embarrass you—and this is nothing I want overheard by the bedpan girls—but do you think a doctor could really predict barrenness from an examination like that? With my own bold plans for replenishing the earth—eight or ten kids *at least*, I used to say, as if the husband part of the deal were a given—I assumed any hereditary defect in that area was something I had a right to be informed of. Mother finally said, "I will tell you what little can be told on the matter when you get engaged yourself." That sure worked out handy. Turns out she didn't have to tell me anything at all.

We almost didn't find Arlin. We could see the blown-up goose out on the ice, but whatever hole or breach there might have been was already frozen back over. It was getting late. The light was all but gone, and we were already down in the shadows of the river bluff. So Dad went ahead and stepped off from the bank to search the ice. I can remember we heard it groan, and you hollered for him to be careful.

"You're a fine one to talk about careful," he said. "If you'd done like I told you to do, we wouldn't be looking for him at all."

That's when he spotted the leather mitten at the downstream end of the pond. It was barely sticking above the surface of one unfrozen spot, next to the dam. That pond was not big, the water not all that deep, and Arlin could hold his breath longer than any of us. But even his lungs had their limit. He got all the way from where he fell through to that one bathtub-sized spot of open water, when his boot snagged in some limbs.

I was only sixteen myself when Arlin drowned—twenty-eight when Rudy Cox proposed. Twelve years. Bishop Sebright said God doesn't number things the way we do. Dad was twenty-two when he married Mother. He had seen things in the Battle of Belleau Wood he couldn't speak of the rest of his life. Mother couldn't make herself tell him about her childbearing prospects until a couple of days before the wedding; she thought he'd call it off. But she misjudged him. He told her that if he'd wanted a brood sow, he would've proposed to one. He said he was just grateful to be alive and doubly grateful to find a woman who would have him. He said he would take children any way the Lord saw fit to give them to him.

If that speech wouldn't melt a girl's heart, I don't know what would. They got married, as scheduled, in the Salt Lake Temple and set about trying to prove the doctor wrong. It took them five years, but they finally managed it. The irony was, after all that waiting and wanting, the timing wasn't particularly opportune. You and I had just made our way into the world from who knows where, and, with a half hour to decide, the folks had adopted us. That's all Mother ever told me. We were three weeks old when she found out she was pregnant. "I've seen this happen," said the same doctor who had predicted it never would. Can you imagine the diapers?

In the fall of 1941, the brand new bishop of the Balford Ward was Hardin Cottrell. He and Enid owned the town's one jewelry store. Arlin was his first funeral. I remember him standing at the podium above the casket, hardly able to get through his closing remarks. He was an uncommonly sensitive man, presiding at an uncommonly sad affair. Even so, as he looked down at the folks, his empathy was like nothing I've seen since, almost as if he were grieving for him and Enid, too. Maybe he was. Less than a week later, their only son, who had just finished Navy boot camp, went down with the *Arizona* at Pearl Harbor. Bishop Cottrell called Arlin's accident a vagary, which was the first time I had heard the word. It seemed a good fit. He said the only way to make peace with vagaries of that kind was through the grace of the Savior. We'd all heard the same all our lives, he said, but now we had to put that grace to the test.

It was a test our family didn't do too well at. In my dream the other night, I heard your voices.

Birthday or not, Loomis, you're just encouraging his strangeness.

I keep telling you, Kaye: that rifle had nothing to do with the boy's drowning.

Do you guys know what a .30/06 will do to a goose at seventy-five yards?

The day you quit school to enlist—a week before Christmas—you said the Army could never send you far enough into the Pacific to get away from Dad's blame, but you could at least get away from him. We were seniors. Oh, I made pretense of urging you to wait until graduation in May, but secretly I envied you leaving. Had I been a boy, I would've done the very same thing. And my eagerness, like yours, would've had nothing to do with patriotism.

You have no idea what it was like. *Oh, we're managing.* That's what you say to people. With so much bad news from the war there at first, the quarreling at home petered out. But the blame didn't; it just scabbed over. There were days Mother and Dad didn't speak ten words to each other. Mealtime was awful. And the only reference he ever made to you was *him*. Any word from *him* lately? So where have they got *him* now?

All we knew was that you had been trained as a sniper and were on some island near New Guinea. That was not a lot of comfort in a house that was already short on it. No wonder no fellas came around to see me. The main reason I was looking forward to having you home alive was for someone to *talk* to. But then you couldn't wait to leave again. Next thing I know, you're married to Nelda and off welding pipeline down in Lamont to save for your beloved dairy. The closest I ever came to a prime of life would've been those next eight years, and they were spent trying to keep our family together instead of starting my own.

Don't misunderstand me, Owen. I admire what you did. If there was ever going to be any forgiveness between you three, *you* were going to have to do the offering. The folks were too proud. Just a week before he was released after twelve long years of bishoping, Hardin Cottrell called you into his office. He said for years after the war, he had a hard time selling a watch or ring to anybody who looked the least bit oriental. "And me the bishop," he said, "telling *others* to forgive!" Then one day in

1950, who should walk into his store but Charlie Nakamura. He wanted a pair of pearl earrings for an anniversary gift. This was the same Charlie Nakamura who had come to Wyoming thirty years earlier and had long since proved himself one of the best farmers and most loyal citizens in the valley. Yet he had had no recourse when his own aunt and uncle were taken from their home in Southern California to spend the war years in one of those tar-paper barracks inside that Heart Mountain camp, not fifteen miles from Charlie's place. "How does a person forgive *that*?" Bishop Cottrell wanted to know. Say what you want about religion, he said, but in the end, only the Lord can pull a thorn of that kind out of a human heart, Charlie Nakamura's, or his, or yours. "Owen," the bishop said, "you are going to have to forgive not being forgiven—for something that wasn't even your fault— or live bitter all your life."

Bishop Cottrell was a good man. But knowing what he knew about thorns in hearts, why didn't he call Dad into the office and talk forgiveness to the one who needed to hear it most? Or Mother? That's a valid question, don't you think? So how was it *you* didn't have to ask it? Not only that, but you actually heeded the counsel and did the forgiving. *How*, I don't know. With ice cream, I guess. That very Sunday night, after talking to Bishop Cottrell, you put your crank-bucket in your truck, told Nelda there was something you had to take care of, long overdue, and came down to the house. Years later you told me that driving into the yard, after staying away so long, was worse than a beach landing.

That decision of yours changed everything. The only part of it that ever bothered me is why you couldn't have mustered such nerve six months earlier, before Rudy Cox married that girl from Sanpete County. You've got to understand. When he walked up the first time at church and asked if he could call on me, I saw light I had never seen and breathed air I had never breathed. I was pushing thirty, and here at last was a fella willing to come to the front porch of *my* house. And he *kept* coming, all fall, enough times evidently to think he knew what he was stepping into.

"So your folks are quirky," he said. "You know anybody whose folks aren't?"

But he didn't know. How could he know? I answered what I answered because I didn't think it was fair to saddle him with our problems. But what I *really* thought—crazy Ivy—was the folks would see what I'd given up for a dozen years on their behalf and would come around and admit how they did not deserve such a daughter! And then I could catch Rudy Cox just before he got on the bus to a sad, lonely life without me and rest in his arms all the way to wherever we were going.

So much for that!

With so many unhappy wives in the world, I have to admit there's worse things than being an old maid. The question that still nags me, though, is whether being one is any harder for having passed up a chance *not* to be one.

This dream was last Thursday night. Friday morning, I'm poking around in the shed for a flower pot, thinking about Arlin, and I drop my hand spade. I bend down to get it, and all of a sudden I'm looking right at it—the very *first* birthday rifle, before the .22s and the shotguns, the one Dad carved from an old joist. Remember the one I'm talking about? There it was, behind my garden shelves, leaning against a wall stud. Think about it: If I hadn't dropped the spade, I would've gone to *my* grave not knowing it was there. I can't believe any of this was chance.

Even on a toy gun, Arlin wanted a scope. He said, "How else am I going to look death in the eye?" Dad said death didn't need the attention and wouldn't a barrel bored with a red-hot spike look a whole lot more authentic than a jerry-rigged piece of pipe anyhow? Arlin was what—seven or eight? Dad sold him on the idea by promising the barrel would always smell like it had just been fired. The boy *loved* guns. When you got out of the service, you said he would've made a lot better sniper than you; you often wondered why he didn't go to war and you drown in the beaver pond. It's no comment on my love for Arlin to say I'm glad you didn't.

No, I have no idea how that carved rifle ended up in my shed, much less how it survived Mother's purge. Do you recall how, after the funeral, she wanted all Arlin's things gone: the big pickle jars full of fangs and rattles and sheddings, sparrows' nests, pheasant eggshells, the "arrowhead" collection—nothing but colored bits of rock—and the raccoon tails strung between rafters up there in that attic bedroom? And deer! He worshipped deer. Skulls. Hooves and dewclaws. Antlers everywhere. "Loomis, he's going to *have* to keep that sort of thing outside." Everywhere he went, he wore an antler tip on a leather shoelace around his neck. He'd hold it up to his head, close his eyes, tell me that's how he could read a deer's mind.

I wish I'd had something to read his. Then maybe we'd know why in heaven's name he defied Dad's instruction for you two to stay together. I can just hear him: "You going to flush those willow bottoms or am I going to have to do it myself?" It's no mystery to *me* why you left him. Anything to be done with the hunt and get back to birthday cake and ice cream in front of the stove. What I never could figure out was why Arlin would send you off to flush the big buck he'd been after all his short life, order you to keep quiet while you're at it, then suddenly decide he couldn't wait another instant without blasting something with his brand new rifle. Even with a stiff breeze, a shot like that would've spooked any mule deer within three miles. You heard it—right? That's what brought you running back to the pond. Poor laggard goose was just looking for a patch of still water for the night, maybe from five thousand feet up thought the pond ice was thinner than it was in the middle. And running to retrieve the bird he'd just blown to smithereens, Arlin apparently thought it was thicker.

Whatever Mother's reasoning, the real guns were the *first* collection to go. She wouldn't have the .30/06 in her sight.

"Let me at least keep his twelve-gauge, Kaye. It meant a lot to him. I'll put it in the shop."

She wouldn't budge; anything with a trigger got given away. The homemade stuff—the weasel trap, the cudgels and tomahawks, all his gigs made of this or that sharpened rod wired to a broom handle—all of it went straight to the burn-pile. And the hat and hunting vest just disappeared. For three or four years before the accident, whenever Mother asked him to let her wash them, Arlin said, "I don't bother your things."

Don't poop out on me here, Owen. Because what I'm getting to next is the truly bizarre part of the dream. Under the name and dates on the headstone, I saw *another* line. As you well know, there *is* no other line. It was big as a billboard and so real I'm half afraid to go out to the cemetery to make sure it's not. Imagine what those bedpan girls would think if they eavesdropped me saying *that*. Wacko Ivy. Then it's shrinks who can't shave normal, padded walls, bars on the windows. But what else can I say except what I saw?

LOOMIS ARLIN TEAGUE

NOV. 28, 1925–NOV. 28, 1941

WHEN ALL IS AT LAST FORGIVEN

It's bad enough to be reminded that your younger brother died at age sixteen, but now he's got an epitaph? And if he's got to have an epitaph, why that one? Thanks to you and your ice cream bucket, all *was* forgiven. Right? A long time ago. It was taken care of. Am I not right in saying that?

I've got half a century to back me up. That was 1953. One Sunday evening you show up at the house with a block of ice and rock salt and your very first half gallon of fresh Jersey cream. You could've just come in, but, no, you knocked. I remember going to the door. You were nervous standing in your own mother's kitchen. And what can be said of the folks' reaction except they were surprised to see you? When you were sure they were both listening, you got right to the point. You said it was about time somebody made ice cream in that house again. And then you asked them to sit down with you at the table. I can repeat what you said next; you were almost whispering: "And don't you think it's about time we let Arlin rest in peace?" You were already on the verge of tears when you turned to Dad. "And for my part of that," you said to him, "I am going to need to ask your forgiveness."

His face! Weather makes a thick skin, but nothing any thicker than what comes of twelve years of bitterness. I didn't really believe what was happening until I heard something like a choking sound and saw Dad biting his lip. For a second, I thought it was anger I was witnessing; that and weeping can look a lot alike. Then it occurred to me his nose was running. I didn't know he had it in him, and I'm not sure Mother did, either. I remember her putting her face in her hands and the tears leaking through her fingers. Ten minutes? Twenty? I don't know. But when that meeting at the kitchen table was over, the block ice had melted a pretty good puddle on the floor. But nobody made a move for a towel or mop. And when you all stood up, Dad actually hugged you. He *hugged* you! Then he turned to Mother. It was something I had never witnessed—my parents embracing. Embracing *and* crying.

It was a miracle—from God. Who can dispute it? I saw, with my own eyes, forgiveness made possible the only way it can be. Not by herbs or yoga or Oprah. This was mercy, grace, and redemption, pure and simple. Bishop Cottrell was right. People can call it what they want, but it's those gifts from the Savior, and nothing else, that mended what was rent, in *your* lives anyway. I know that.

But what about your twin sister off to the side? With the long night finally over, I should've been dancing for joy. But I wasn't. In fact, the whole scene, sweet and awkward as it was, made me about half sore. *I'm* the one who ended up with the mopping, that night and all twelve years before it. And by the way, Ivy, thanks a bunch.

Six months! If only God could've seen fit to bestow this one miracle the fall before instead of the next spring. If only you could've come over with your ice cream bucket that much earlier! Of course, you *had* your marriage and kids. Six months would've been just before my twenty-eighth birthday; it would've been perfect.

That's the birthday Mr. Rudy Cox gave me a corn flakes box wrapped with butcher paper. Inside was a blue scarf. He was twenty-six, two years younger than I was. That's not such a difference; nevertheless, I asked him if my vintage bothered him. He said, "Maturity has its advantages, Ivy." The rascal. I knew what he was leading up to, had prayed and waited for it a long time. But at *that* point there had been no amazing grace in the Teague household. And no prospects for such made even a girl of my vintage say things she didn't really mean. It *still* hurts. I didn't think the boy would step off the porch that last time and never come back. Next I heard he'd married the girl from Sanpete County.

Dream dreams! Of course Bishop Clive Sebright didn't *say* spinsters. "Righteous unmarried sisters" is what he said—what all my bishops have said. And I've lived through a lot of them in eighty-four years. When I turned fifty, Bishop Frett Maxwell Jr. promised that any worthy desire denied me in mortality would be made up for in the hereafter. Okay by me; I would've liked prettier toes and a reason to wear a nightie. Twenty years later—though I'd long since made peace with bunions and flannel pajamas—Emery Bingham told me the same thing. I had him in Cub Scouts! At least I had the satisfaction of seeing my lesson on good manners take. Every Mother's Day during his tenure—six or seven years, whatever it was—when the Aaronic Priesthood boys brought the flowers into the chapel to pass out, Bishop Bingham stood at the pulpit and made sure every adult female got one, whether her womb had borne fruit or not. He said *all* women were nurturers. You'd think by then I could've heard such words without crying.

I've never liked bothering bishops with my problems, but with the wooden rifle and the dream and the epitaph, I had to make an exception. So after church today, I asked Bishop Brierley what *he* thought about spinsters and their dreams. He said, "Are we talking general-all-of-you or specific-Ivy?" That sounds just like him. He's Balford's new chief of police, moved up here last year from Denver. He comes to see you all the time.

He heard me out. Then he said, "Your brother Owen is one in a thousand." Well, I knew that already. There was a long stretch of him tapping the desk with his big fingers before he finally remarked that hard feelings must be Satan's strategy for people who can't be tempted to much else. Of course, I assumed he was talking about you and the folks. Then he said, "And your Bishop Cottrell was dead-on about the remedy for that." He looked at me so hard he almost made me squirm. "And if we're at all willing, Jesus will point us to it any way he can, including your dream."

There was no use playing coy with the man. Down in Denver, he was a detective. If you were hiding serious sin, he would not be the man to sit across a desk from. So I went ahead and admitted that, being human, I was hardly immune to rancor. But I assured him that, in time, I *had* made peace with everybody involved. I told him there's no use crying over what can't be changed, right? Do you know what he did? He nodded—that's it. Didn't say a word. But I got the feeling he was nodding without agreeing.

This place they've got you dying in is just up the street from my house. On warm afternoons I can look out my bedroom window and see the wheelchairs parked on the "veranda." That's what Muriel calls it, but she knows better than anybody that the word is all whitewash. You don't see dotards in wheelchairs taking in cool breezes or sipping lemonade; they've got all they can do just to draw oxygen. And if I look for very long in that direction, I'm slumped in a chair right there with them, barely drawing it myself.

It's funny. I've never felt like I knew enough about how I got into this world, but thanks to you, I know more than I want to about how I'm likely to get out of it. But frankly, the bodily deterioration doesn't worry me like it used to. No, I don't much like the idea of someone like Muriel having to diaper me, good as she is; or, if I get to stay in my house, shriveling three days in a cold bathtub before the paperboy starts asking questions. But it's going to happen one way or the other. I just know this: Wherever we're going, we'll go there without wheelchairs and sickbeds.

I've got other things to worry about tonight. Bishop Brierley asked do I fully understand what Jesus did for me. Eighty-four years of life on this planet, church every Sunday of it, I better hope I do. I didn't mean to be testy, but of *course* I understand what Jesus did. The bishop said, "Just wondering." Then he asked did I know how that worked—not just for people who have to forgive a wrong, but maybe for those who have to forgive a right. It sounds like a riddle, but I knew exactly what that foxy old detective meant. I've just never thought of it like that before. He had things more figured out than I realized. "Hard as it was losing Rudy Cox," he said, "who and what you were blaming for it was even harder."

Ah, Owen. I wanted in the worst way to feel indignant, but all I ended up feeling was found out. Eighty-four years, and I was so tired and shameful I wanted to crawl in a cave. I have known better than I have done. Bishop Brierley said an amazing thing. He said it's true we've got to feel a good many of our own stripes before we're healed with the Lord's, but that one doesn't automatically lead to the other. Then he looked at me and said—and he really was very nice about it: "Ivy, I think maybe you've been nursing your stripes long enough."

I was hoping, after visiting with him, I could go back to the puzzle book by my TV chair and keeping up with my dozen different pills every day, and that would be the end of it. But that's not going to work. I never wanted to feel hard toward *you*, of all people. You're my twin, now and forever. But I did feel that way; I truly did. Why a person should resent what I've resented, I don't know. But I *did*. And now sitting here at your bedside, thinking about what Bishop Brierley said, I am sorry beyond sorry for that. Life is too short and too long both.

Even if you're as close to lung-rattling as Muriel seems to think, I know she's right: I know you can hear me. And if you can hear me, maybe you can forgive me—you and Jesus both. There's hope just hoping for such. I wish I was going with you and we could meet Arlin and the folks at the same time. Meanwhile, I will envy your reunion and will think hard on whether this envy is right or wrong. According to the hospice ladies, rattling is the sure sign. *It won't be much longer now.* That's how they say it—with a very soothing voice.

TURTLE FEATHERS

B UT YOU SAID YOUR UNCLE TALKED TO THE FHA GUY
and Salt Lake was a sure thing."

"It's a government job, Brynne; you've got to go where they send you."

"To Balford, Wyoming—two days after Thanksgiving? And not a word to me about it?"

"What do you call dinner at a place like this?"

"That's nine hundred miles away."

"*Five* hundred," Tate Rigney said, tugging at the knot of a borrowed yellow tie. "I don't know why you always have to blow things out of proportion."

"What am I blowing out of proportion? Us?" She looked at him and waited. When he didn't answer, she said, "Three years since you graduated, Tate. Three years talking about a crummy job market. So, okay, you were looking for just the right fit. But at the very least, I thought that meant something close to both our families, something in the general area."

"I'm not turning this down if that's what you're asking."

"What I'm asking is about you and me." She studied the fork in her hand, then set it on the tablecloth beside her twenty-dollar entree. She waited, again. Then, in a very low voice, she said, "For you, my miscarriage was just a lucky relief; I know that. But for me . . . I wasn't raised to do it this way."

He wouldn't meet her eye.

"I wish you'd come with me to see the bishop. If he knew we were serious, that we had plans—"

"I've told you, Brynne: I just don't see how this is any of your bishop's business. And I already know what the Mormon church is going to say about us being together."

"'Together?' Do you remember the very first thing you said when I told you the test was positive?"

He didn't answer.

"You said, 'Have you considered *your* options?'"

He pushed his overpriced plate toward the center of the table. "We've been over this a hundred times. I'm just not as ready for this as you are."

"So when? You're almost thirty, Tate. And you always seem ready enough to sneak off to your uncle's cabin." She was crying now. "My dad was twenty-one when he proposed to my mother. Just home from a mission—no car, no money, and no degree in anything like 'Finance Systems'—but he asked, and she said yes. That's what ready is, Tate. And I bet they didn't have mice in *their* mattress."

He tugged harder at the knot of the borrowed yellow tie. "You promised you wouldn't pressure me on this anymore."

"Oh, I get it," she said, wiping streaked mascara with her nice cloth napkin. "I have to promise, and you don't."

⟹ ⟸

On a Monday morning twelve years earlier, in the spring of the new millennium, a man named Toribio Gomez rolled down Balford's main street for the first time. He had come here because it was close to Yellowstone Park, a place he was obsessed with. Even in a town settled by Mormons, his old white Suburban was less conspicuous for its Virgin Mary hood ornament and bad muffler than for its yellow tailgate. Behind the front seat of that Suburban were two canvas panniers full of cash, and under the driver's side of that seat was a short-barreled, twelve-gauge pump shotgun. Toribio was fifty-two years old, and he was by himself.

When Gorrell Vanderfisk got to his real estate office that morning at seven-thirty, Toribio, all five and a half feet of him, was waiting by the door. Studying the stubble and uncombed hair, the shabby denim coat and tennis shoes laced with packing string, Gorrell passed certain judgments. Then, during the inquiry about bargain properties in the country and the approximate driving distance to Yellowstone—made in barely understandable English—he passed others. But when one of those hands, missing its ring finger, reached into the coat's big flap pocket and pulled out a rubber-banded loaf of cash, then did it a second time, Gorrell Vanderfisk was persuaded the man was neither stewbum nor crank.

By noon of that April morning in 2000, one of the panniers was empty, and Toribio was the owner of twenty-five acres of sagebrush on a bench south of town, in the foothills of the treeless McCoullough Peaks. The property, Gorrell Vanderfisk assured him, was not without improvements: a charitably named double-wide with a scabbed-on porch, clothesline and garden plot, milk cow stanchion and pump house, and a hand-dug hole about a third as big around and deep as it would have had to be to accommodate a sometime intended bomb shelter.

"And if I remember correctly," Gorrell Vanderfisk said, "there's an orchard."

The locals knew the place as Ashwurm's Last Stand, named in affectionate mockery for the man who had first thought to park that particular double-wide on that particular patch of northwest Wyoming. Three decades earlier, Orlin Ashwurm had himself come to Balford, in a converted school bus, to hole up with his large family against the scourges of the last days. Over the next few years, he made a name for himself as a predictor of doom. Then, at the town's Fourth of July picnic in 1975, he publicly declared that America's Bicentennial the following year would usher in the Second Coming. When it didn't and his already thin credibility evaporated, he packed up his canned food, along with his wife Dove and those of his eight children who weren't shamed into striking out on their own, and pointed the school bus toward Chihuahua, Mexico, and aquifers that would survive Armageddon.

At almost exactly the same time, in a pueblo called Julimes, in that same part of Mexico, twenty-eight-year-old Toribio Gomez filled his pockets with tortillas and raisins, hung a plastic water jug from a shoulder strap made of a bicycle's inner tube, and took up a map with the route to El Paso marked in grease pen.

"But why, *mi querido,* why?" Toribio's *prometida* asked on the eve of his departure.

Because he did not want to be, in his old age, another poor *campesino* with a poor *campesino* wife. Opportunity to be something else lay northward, across the border.

"But I'll be back for you," he promised, "when I'm a rich *dueño.*"

⇒   ⇐

Which is what he had long since become by late November of 2012. In a dozen years he had expanded westward and now owned close to two hundred acres of foothills sagebrush. Somewhere at the far edge of that mostly uncleared acreage, he lived in a *hacienda* of his own making. From there, he managed his many rental properties, the oldest and biggest being Ashwurm's Last Stand.

On the Wednesday after Thanksgiving, a maid named Armida noted, for the fourth morning in a row, the little Toyota pickup truck with the Utah license plate parked in front of room 118 of the Balford Inn. Under its fiberglass camper shell, the truck bed held a hiker's backpack, golf clubs, a board and sail for windsurfing, and a pair of snow skis, poles, boots. The gear had been hurriedly loaded. She found Tate Rigney at one of the three little tables in the continental breakfast lobby, poring over the meager *For Rent* section of the latest semiweekly issue of the *Clarion*. A Styrofoam bowl of Sugar Pops rested beside an open laptop computer with a dead screen. The internet connection had lasted just long enough to confirm that there had been no e-mail message from Brynne.

"We don't got so good signal here," Armida said. She paused, studying him, then said, "And some landlords, they don't advertise none."

Late that afternoon, following Armida's map, sketched on a coffee filter, Tate crossed the Shoshone River south of Balford, went five miles on the washboard gravel of McCoullough Road, then turned in at Ashwurm's Last Stand. Thirty yards farther, in the grassless yard of the double-wide, he brought his truck to a stop just behind the Suburban's yellow tailgate and a rear window hatch with no glass in it. On one side of the Suburban was a pump house and, on the other, a bomb shelter hole of uncertain depth. For many seasons, the hole had caught the overflow—including a brewery's quantity of aluminum cans—from an off-plumb burn barrel tethered to an even more off-plumb steel post.

Since the *dueño* of the double-wide was nowhere to be seen, nothing like introductory pleasantries got in the way of a hard-eyed scrutiny of its faults, including duct-taped window fractures, fallen skirting, an insufficient number of cinder-block piers, and a slack guy cable at each end of both frame beams. "The wind in that part of Wyoming would blow the stripe off a skunk," Uncle Mont had said during the loading of the Toyota. The roof of the scabbed-on porch was more tar patches than shingles, and the floor sagged like an alkali bog. "And you really got out of the restaurant without telling her about ditching the Salt Lake gig?"

Tate climbed out of his truck. The cold defied the afternoon's sunshine. In shaded corners, last night's inch of snow had not melted. Beneath the closest of the porch's bowed joists, two cats fed on the contents of a shredded sack of dog food. They were big and ugly. Depending on the fickle reflection of light, their cat eyes alternated between sullen wariness and a sightless green glow. "Man," Uncle Mont had said, "if I could've pulled off a poker face like that, I wouldn't be staring sixty in the face and paying alimony times two."

Not until he had mounted the rickety steps and looked away from the porch did Tate notice the orchard. Its closest border lay thirty yards beyond the pump house, southwest of the double-wide's front door. Unlike her husband, Dove Ashwurm had had some faith in the future—at least enough to plant apple trees. And the orchard wasn't the last of the property's features. Visible just beyond the leafless branches of a tree on its periphery was the top of a corner post and a swatch of woven wire. Tate was straining to follow the wire with his eye when, suddenly, from that very direction, a man appeared.

It was Toribio Gomez.

With a hustling, slightly pigeon-toed gait, he covered the distance to the pump house. From one hand swung the bail of a white plastic bucket. At the door of the pump house, he gently set the bucket down. Then, deviating only to soccer-kick a stray beer can toward the bomb shelter hole, he came on toward the porch. He was short and barrel-chested, and his financial successes during his twelve and a half years in Balford had not altered his taste in clothing. Now, though, along with the baggy denim coat and Goodwill pants and tennis shoes, there was a big straw cowboy hat with a long, charcoal-colored feather stuck in its band.

When he finally spoke, from fifteen yards, his words made a curious greeting:

"So why you come here, U-Tah?"

For an instant Tate supposed him to mean something he didn't, and he felt exposed.

"You like Yellow-stone?" When Tate didn't answer, the questions came faster: "You send from Marisol? Isabel maybe?" Then the *dueño* caught himself and, finger-stabbing the air with each word, said, "No, no, no. You Balford Inn, right? *La buenísima* Armida. She ve-ry good for business, no?" Practicing his soccer moves a second time, Toribio kicked a frozen dog turd at the feral cats. They did not flinch. Skipping up the rickety porch steps and fishing for a door key in his coat of many pockets, he said, "You like inside ve-ry much."

Nothing in the five-minute tour of the place supported such an assertion. Not the kitchen counter swollen and bubbled from faucet seepage, not caulking like chewed gum, not a toilet bowl that hadn't known a thorough scrubbing since Dove Ashwurm, not the pervasive smell of a bad potato. And all that was palace-grade compared to the master bedroom. In the middle of its red shag carpet—puzzle-pieced, hatchet-trimmed, and anchored at the edges with lath and six-penny nails—lay the room's only furnishing. No bed frame, no box spring, no headboard. Just a king-sized mattress like an island amid sunflower shells, ashtrays haggled from beer cans, several well-thumbed girlie magazines, mouse droppings, and a pair of boxer shorts. Not to mention dog hair thick enough to rake.

Tate's grimace was not lost on the rich *dueño*.

"Last guy," Toribio admitted, with enough head shaking to agitate his feather, "he no good renter. *Baboso. Flojo. Malsano.* Leave things ve-ry *sucio.*"

It was at that moment they both noticed, protruding from beneath one corner of the island, the glossy jumbo condom box—smashed flat, empty. The room grew close.

After a few moments, Toribio smiled lopsidedly and, pointing his chin toward the hard-ridden mattress, said, "But he don't never slept cold." As a sort of afterthought, he asked, "You got any woman?"

Almost a full week and no calls, no e-mails, no text messages on the cell phone's little screen. No. No woman.

"*Bueno*, this be *perfecto* for you," Toribio said. "And only five hundred a month. Ve-ry cheap. Many oil workers ask place to rent. Ve-ry busy in Badger Basin again. But I give for you, U-Tah. What you think?"

The place was squalid, worse even than that U of U frat house his junior year, when, at age twenty-four, he begged reinstatement from the Sigma Chi folks after dropping out to follow that girl named Danielle to Reno. By then, though, it was the underclassmen who had to make the place ready for inspection.

Squalid and overpriced. But it was a nice, long distance from another talk with Brynne about their future.

Finally, he nodded.

Back outside in the chill of late afternoon, Toribio flung open the Suburban's passenger door. From the glove compartment he dug a folded contract, dog-eared receipt booklet, and a red Bic pen. That's when Tate noticed the sewed-over finger socket.

"You leave before year," Toribio said, "you still pay. *Comprende*, U-Tah?

He did, or at least he thought he did. He took the pen and signed: *Tate DeLane Rigney.*

Otherwise, he never used the middle name. It always reminded him of that old Mormon scoutmaster back home. Neal Delozier. He was completely bald, had a wart over one ear and big liver spots on his forehead and crown. No sooner had the non-Mormon Rigneys moved into that house in Spanish Fork than Brother Delozier was hauling over buckets of garden stuff and trying to get Tate to join his Mormon scout troop. Brother Delusion. That's what his dad called him despite accepting his cucumbers and tomatoes and agreeing, with affected conviction, that what the world needed most was boys better prepared for the burdens of manhood.

The Bic was drying up. Tate handed it back to his four-fingered landlord, then pulled out his wallet and said, "About those cats."

"Electric already on," Toribio said. "*Got* to stay on, every time. Pump need electric. You put name in Ralston Light and Power, okay? I call them—they wait for you *mañana*."

"Listen," Tate said, "I hate cats. I'm allergic to them. *Comprende?*"

Toribio wouldn't meet his eye. He hustled around to the driver's side and opened the Suburban's other front door. "*Sí, comprendo,* because you speak-a ve-ry good Spanish," he said, smiling, as he reached beneath the seat. "You need ve-ry good Animal Control." Just as Tate rounded the vehicle's front end, the *dueño* rounded the rear, chuckling as he went. "*Ven aca, gatitos gorditos,*" he said in a lilting voice. "Come to Papi."

For several more of Toribio's tip-toeing steps, the Suburban blocked Tate's view. By the time it didn't block his view, the short-barreled twelve-gauge was already being aimed from a kneeling position, not fifteen feet from the shredded dog food sack.

K-poom! K-poom! K-poom!

After one final breech-click of the pump action, quiet settled again over Ashwurm's Last Stand—except for some kind of commotion on the far side of the orchard, in the direction of that corner post and woven wire. Without gathering the spent shells, Toribio stood, hurried back to the Suburban, and stowed the gun. Then, reaching through the glassless rear-window hatch, he grabbed a half-handled square shovel and jabbed it upright in the weed-covered fill-dirt at the rim of the bomb shelter hole. Turning to Tate, he said, "No more allergy, eh, U-Tah?"

⬆ ⬅

From age twenty-eight, when he nearly drowned crossing the Rio Grande an hour after a rare cloudburst upstream near Ciudad Juárez, Toribio became well acquainted with the work available in the land of opportunity to one of his skin color and accent—fruit picking in Texas, beet thinning in California, hod carrying in Seattle. Eventually he wound up on a pulling unit in the oil fields outside Casper, Wyoming.

One hot noon break in August of 1985, nine years after the near-drowning, the pulling-unit foreman flung his half-eaten sandwich into the scrub of the Wyoming plain. "Treebie," he said, "I will buy you a six-pack of whatever beverage you name if you'll let me have a bite of that Mexican thing you're eating."

Toribio produced a big pocket knife, divided the taquito, and proffered the slightly larger portion.

The foreman sniffed at it, stuck it in his mouth, chewed tentatively, then with increasing gusto. "Mm, that's delicious. What's in it?"

Toribio considered for only a moment.

"Ve-ry good spice-meat. Cook two days in special fire pit *mejicano* with mesquite wood. Make ve-ry *delicioso*."

What Toribio didn't disclose was the source of his spice-meat—outdated grocery-store chicken, butcher scraps, even the occasional freshly road-killed deer or antelope. Nor did he disclose the actual cooking method—a ten-dollar crockpot crowded onto the kitchen counter of a flea-bag apartment shared with eight or ten others of his skin color and accent. The meat's flavor derived mostly from peppers and chilies. *Just* enough tabasco, cayenne, jalapeño, maybe even a fleck of habanero to vanquish gaminess without scorching the palate. Mix the spice-meat with a little cheese, roll tight in a corn tortilla, half again the diameter of a cigar, then deep-fry until crispy—and nobody in his right mind would ever again stoop to white bread and bologna.

"How about tomorrow you make a couple of these for me?" the foreman asked. "I'm guessing you're a Corona man."

Sí, he was fond of the nectar *cerveza*, but Toribio gave the foreman to understand that he was even fonder of money—say, fifty cents *cada uno*?

"You've got yourself a deal."

Word spread. Rig operators, welders, roustabouts, pump-truck drivers. By and by even the folks in clean hardhats and safety glasses. "I hear you make a mean tamale, fella," said a chemical engineer who didn't get out in the sun much. So long as money exchanged hands, customers could call Toribio's creations anything they wanted to.

First one insulated lunch box packed full every day and carried to work, then two. Then the lunch boxes got bigger. Stacked like tiny cordwood, that many foil-wrapped taquitos stayed warm for hours. In the early days of the enterprise, they sold two or four per customer, but before long, the most common unit was a dozen, discounted to five dollars. Within half a year, business was thriving. There wasn't fifteen cents' worth of ingredients in one of Toribio's taquitos, and the labor, for someone who had cut his teeth on a hoe handle, was child's play, to be managed in the evenings and wee hours. Yet with each sale, he tripled his money.

On the day the latch jammed on the sucker rod elevator, the planned career change became more urgent.

"Hammer!" the operator yelled up from the floor of the pulling unit. "Use a hammer!"

But standing in the rod basket sixty feet up the derrick, Toribio couldn't hear the instruction above the roar of the rig. And even if he had heard it, he didn't have a hammer. In the making do without one, his glove's little finger was mangled, the one next to it pinched off.

"Too bad about your hand," said the well service representative who showed up after outpatient surgery. "As a token of the company's concern for your welfare, I am authorized to offer you, by way of compensation, two thousand dollars. And on a personal note," he added, "I surely hope none of this gets in the way of you rolling those tostados. I've got to tell you, Mr.

Treebio—I thought I'd just try me one today, since I was in town, and they are a *treat*."

"No," said Toribio, whose head was remarkably clear despite the numbing of his knuckles, "no get in way. But maybe circumstance pay for ten thousand. And I no talk to no lawyer about you hire *hispanos* with no social security *numero* for ve-ry dangerous work."

Within a year, he was no longer risking digits to jockey fifty-foot sticks of sucker rod; he and his crew were selling fifteen hundred taquitos a day in Casper and all the little oil towns—Midwest, Natrona, Alcova, Glenrock—within a fifty-mile radius. And he was no longer sharing an apartment with three times as many human beings as it was designed for. He had rented locker space at a butcher's shop and a house with a big kitchen, a garden plot, and a two-car garage easily wired for a commercial roaster and two deep fryers.

"That meat," customer after customer declared, "I've never tasted anything like it."

Thus was kindled Toribio's fondest dream: He wanted to find some cheap property somewhere close to Yellowstone and raise meat animals to supply his own taquito filling.

As for Toribio's crew, there was no shortage of cheap help. Woman after woman couldn't resist mixing business and pleasure, and hoping the mix would somehow yield marriage. But such a yield was the furthest thing from the mind of a man who left a *novia* in Julimes when he was twenty-eight and did not manage his promised return until he was almost forty and nursing a hand wrapped in gauze.

⇒   ⇐

On his first night at Ashwurm's Last Stand, lying in the stud box of the former tenant with only a self-inflating backpacker's mattress between his sleeping bag and plywood subflooring, Tate added new justifications to a list well rehearsed on the long road from Salt Lake to Balford.

He had been hustled. No steam cleaner on earth would have been equal to the filth and stink ground into the fiber of that red shag. For the subflooring to be so freckled with stains, something pretty bad must have oozed through the carpet backing. Slaver? Urine? Bile? And the mattress was an embarrassment—gone in the springs, stained on both sides, probably full of nits. The rest of the carpet in the place was no better, should have been pulled up years ago. And contrary to the landlord's claims, the water filter on the kitchen faucet was not brand new, the toilet did not flush with any particular vigor, and the propane tank set in the sagebrush north of double-wide was *not* almost full. Until a truck from the gas company could get out here tomorrow, there would be no hot water, no cooking, no furnace.

So it was no compromise of warmth to leave the bedroom window ajar, the better to hear the occasional popping of the fire in the bomb shelter hole. With so much to burn—carpet, trash, mattress, the shoveled-up remains of the feral cats—the flames had made a pleasing sight under the late November stars.

"Any fix you want," Toribio had said at the signing of the contract. "Just save *recibo* paper; I take off rent next time. Move-in special."

Of course, when he said that, the landlord was probably thinking of a little rental carpet cleaner at the grocery store or a jug of roach spray. Not incineration. But why should Tate have to mention his intentions when Toribio was so sly about not mentioning his—at least not until after the signing with the spotty red pen? As it turned out, there was a specific chore of maintenance expected of the tenant. To explain it, the landlord had led the way to the squat eight-by-eight pump house, whose cinder block walls were insulated with straw bales stacked two high.

"You know emu birds?" Toribio had asked, retrieving the white plastic bucket he had been carrying when he came out of the orchard. He tilted it so as to reveal its secret. Cushioned on a wadded gunny sack was an egg like no egg Tate had ever seen. It was a deep blue-green—the same length and girth as the miniature plastic footballs cheerleaders hurled into the bleachers, but rounded at each end.

Toribio had entrusted the bucket to Tate and turned to a pump house door just his height. The outward swinging of the door revealed one side of a glass case crowded right up to the jamb. It was an incubator. The sawhorses it rested on were themselves crowded around the water pump apparatus that gave the building its name. Inside the incubator, a heat lamp shone on a whole clutch of the oblong green eggs. The lamp's power cord stretched upward, overtight, to an outlet in the light-bulb receptacle.

Gently, delicately, Toribio lifted the incubator's lid and nestled the new egg among its brightly lit mates.

"Emu eggs take ve-ry careful," he whispered, sucking breath through his teeth. "I buy hen birds all-ready to hatch many new chicks." He pointed beneath the sawhorses, to a chick-sized plastic waterer, an aluminum feeder, a half sack of scratch, and a brooder lamp with a rusty cowl. "When eggs hatch, you keep here, just hang other light from any-where and give food and water."

Six hours later, lying in his sleeping bag on plywood sub-flooring, Tate savored his response to Toribio's sidling indenture:

"Wait a minute, *amigo.* I'm not babysitting your eggs."

"No baby-sit," Toribio had said, offended. "Emu eggs no need no baby-sit. Put in case; is all. If egg hatch, hang lamp, put food and water; is all. Hen birds no need no baby-sit *tampoco.* Ve-ry strong, ve-ry tough. Every-thing automatic. I show you."

And *that* is how they had finally ended up at the corner post on the other side of the orchard, staring through the mesh of six-foot-high woven wire at a dozen of the weirdest birds on the planet.

"How they look?" Toribio asked. "Ve-ry beauty-ful, no? Like *tortugas* with feathers, no?"

Tate had never heard the word, but, looking at the big birds, he knew instantly what it meant; he had just made the same unlikely comparison. Add two more legs, shorten them and the neck by a couple of feet, and that strange head, shaped like a question mark, would look right at home poking out of a shell.

But turtles weren't nearly as skittish. Ten minutes after the shotgun blasts, those beauty-ful feathers still hadn't settled on the hump backs. And turtles knew the value of silence. These birds made a constant noise, more machine than animal—like the monotonous pull-start trill of a balky chainsaw.

"No need no baby-sit," Toribio had said for the tenth time. "I leave grain food in *cajónes*"—he pointed to two plywood feeders—"and they no need nothing for two weeks, when I come or send some-body. *Ni* water *tampoco*"—he pointed to an aluminum trough in the corner—"be-cause everything auto-matic. You just only watch eggs while I gone. Only few more coming, and with eggs in glass, I hatch ma-ny more birds."

Thinking of his snow skis, Tate said, "My contract doesn't say anything about this."

"Is in fine print," Toribio said, smiling ambiguously. "You sign, you no can leave early without pay me."

"Maybe we'll just find out what a lawyer sees in the fine print," Tate said.

"No need no lawyer," Toribio said. Then, moving his hands to suggest a set of scales, he said, "I help you; you help me. *Igual,* no? Any fix you want, you save *recibo* paper. You live alone yourself—no wife, no *hijos,* no problem. You find emu egg, you put in glass, keep warm. Is all. Give food and water to baby chick. Is all. What you think, U-Tah?"

He thought this: He didn't know any lawyers in Balford, Wyoming.

For a long time after the yellow tailgate had disappeared up the road, after the chugging of the bad muffler had faded, Tate stood staring through the wire mesh. The sun had started its winter slide to the horizon, and the late afternoon air was raw. Only gradually did he realize two more details of his new tenancy: First, starting tomorrow, the electricity needed to incubate the eggs and pump the water trough full would be charged to his meter; and second, the landlord had left no way to get in touch with him. He had hinted that he lived close by, but hints were nothing to hold to in an emergency.

At that point, a big hen had stork-stepped toward the fence. When she got within two feet, she stopped, then stretched her neck toward the upper strands of the woven wire. Up close, the long, scaled legs didn't look so spindly. They were stout as pick handles and made spear tips of those overgrown middle toes. Tate regarded the whiskered ostrich head and the beak dripping grain ration. The bird's nictitating membranes had slid open across the bulbous *tortuga* eyeballs, exposing him now to the full scrutiny of the dark pupils: You have to promise, and he doesn't, Tate Rigney. It's in *el contrato*.

Any fix you want! It was no respect for orderliness or hygiene that had motivated the purging of the double-wide. He wouldn't be coerced.

The sleeping bag was snug. Somewhere deep in the foothills, a coyote yipped. Tomorrow he would establish his jogging route, buy groceries, get squared away. He shifted on the camping mattress and laced his fingers behind his head. He was sleepy, but that emu noise was incessant—like Wal-Mart propaganda broadcast from those pillar-mounted TVs the nightshift had to listen to. "Degree or not," Brynne had said, "I don't see why you can't stick with *some* kind of job more than two weeks while you're looking for something better." What that bird noise really sounded like was the warm-up flams of half a dozen drummers, or maybe a mallet riff. He hadn't wanted to camp with Brother

Delusion's scout troop, but camping was a reason to give his dad for quitting after only half a semester in the percussion section of the Spanish Fork Dons. The strategy worked. "A few survival skills might come in handy," Tate's dad had said. "It never hurts to know how to build a fire."

The sleeping bag was very snug. When he closed his eyes, he saw Brynne's face, remembered her body on the mattress in the cabin. Condoms and pregnancy tests—the boxes were almost the same size. "Set a few traps next time you're up there, would you?" Uncle Mont had asked. "I swear, those poison baits are *increasing* the fertility of my rodent population."

He had bought the sleeping bag one semester instead of the textbooks required in one of his business classes. It cost almost three hundred dollars. One of the books was written by the professor. What a racket. Tate got by mooching or guessing on the multiple-choice tests. You had to admire guys who figured out ways to make a lot of easy money. The sleeping bag was goose down, rated to five below zero. He was too tired to get up and latch the window. If faucet drips and wall clocks and frat brothers bedded with girlfriends could be tuned out in the night, so could the drumming of emus.

= =

"So what do you call ten FHA officers chained to a block of concrete at the bottom of the ocean?" asked District Manager Kemp Godwin the next Tuesday.

"A good start?" Tate ventured, without hesitation. It was his second morning on the job in the little FHA building across from Balford Tire.

Kemp Godwin was fifty-four, had started most of the last quarter century's worth of work days with a joke. Before FHA, on his first job out of college, his good humor had blessed the atmosphere of an F.W. Woolworth store in Denver. Now, on the fourth day of December, 2012, he stood in the narrow hallway between two little offices—one with a window and one without—and yelled out to the lobby: "Danajean? Did you tell him the answer?" The question was directed to the secretary behind a computer screen decorated with cardboard reindeer antlers.

"She's innocent," Tate said. "I've heard the same joke about lawyers and tax auditors and—no offense—Mormons."

"Now you know where our profession ranks," Kemp Godwin said. "Maybe you and I should go into business for ourselves—like your landlord. Did Armida mention the taquitos?"

"She wouldn't even tell me where he lives."

"Just up the road from you," Kemp said. "All that property above you—he owns it. Every year he buys up more. Little house in the big sagebrush."

"You been there?"

"Toribio's compound? You kidding? It'd take CIA clearance to get anywhere close to the center of that place. But I did fly over it one time in my brother Siler's ultralight. It's there all right. He wants to raise the taquito meat here, close to his beloved Yellowstone—I don't think he's ever been up there—then truck it to Casper. Casper's where he does all the roasting and rolling and deep-frying. Sells these taquitos all over the state. And now Montana, I understand. Wherever the workers are. Mostly oil still—drilling rigs and pulling units—but he's expanded to highway crews. Sends his little vendor trucks all over the place. And get this—it's all hispanic gals do the work. The guy's no dummy. Couple of cute Latinas show up right at lunch time in the middle of nowhere with a wagon load of hot taquitos, and these hardhats—the majority of them hispanic themselves these days—they'll fork over the money."

"All those women—you sure it's just taquitos he's selling?"

"Hard to believe, I grant you. But why *else* would he give a flip about cheap meat? First, it's chinchilla rabbits, hundreds of them. Then some kind of Chinese cold-climate wonder pig.

Then, of course, the goats. He's tried so many kinds of animals, he's run out of room at his compound. Everything takes a different kind of accommodation. That's why you've got Big Bird in your back yard."

"Rabbit meat in a taquito?" Tate asked.

"You watch," said Kemp Godwin. "Next thing it'll be domesticated possum or muskox out your window. Might *have* to be since the coyotes. Six or eight months ago, they got into the goats while Toribio was on the road again—Dubois or Bozeman or somewhere. One of his lady friends was supposed to be guarding the pasture, I heard, but how do you keep coyotes out? It was right when they were dropping their babies, too. Hamstrung the big ones, tore the throats out of the little ones. Not a survivor in the bunch. That's what always happens. He's never around. If meat were the keystone of *your* business enterprise, wouldn't you tend to it?"

Tate looked at his new boss and said, "How many lady friends does this guy have?"

"Now that, my friend, is a question that interests this town even more than what the man's putting in his taquitos."

"And he's never gotten serious with any of them?"

Kemp Godwin laughed, stepped into the office with a window, and slid into his swivel chair as if into a cockpit.

"What's so funny?" Tate asked.

"From what I hear of your charm with the barmaid at the one watering hole in our little town, you are a fine one to be asking about serious."

⇒ ⇐

The severed finger wasn't the only injury suffered when the latch jammed on the sucker rod elevator. Recoiling from the clash and the sight of a gloved finger that didn't pull free when the gloved hand did, Toribio flailed for balance. In the flailing, one boot slipped on the oil-slicked floor of the rod basket. The knee twisted, but the ankle broke.

So it was only with the help of crutches that he climbed out of a recently purchased Suburban, a week after the accident, and approached the gate of a strange house in Julimes. "Dulce?" a neighbor from the old *barrio* had said. "Her parents are dead, and she has moved."

It was after ten o'clock on a night in early August of 1986. Against the sheet-metal gate of a dark house in the new *barrio,* the rubber tip of the crutch sounded clearly in the night.

Tap-tap-tap.

He waited, then used the crutch's aluminum leg on the top spar of the gate frame.

Clang-clang-clang.

A light came on. The front door opened.

"*Quien es?*" came the voice he had not heard in many years.

"*Tu prometido.*"

He heard a gasp, then bare feet running on a sidewalk. Then she was at the gate, fumbling with the latch. When the gate swung open, he saw, in moonlight, her face and thin nightgown. What she saw was the cast on the left foot—the one not needed to press a gas pedal in the thirteen hundred miles just traveled—and the hand wrapped with blood-spotted gauze.

She did not fall into his arms. She did not weep with joy and relief. She did not touch the stubbled face tenderly. When she asked what had happened to him—"*Que te pasó?*"—she wasn't referring to his injuries.

He had just started an explanation that pretended otherwise—how so much driving violated the doctor's orders, how, even resting on the steering wheel, the hand throbbed, how the dressing should have been changed somewhere between Trinidad and Albuquerque—when there was another voice from the doorway of the house.

"Who is it, *mi querida?*" a man asked.

Toribio looked at Dulce.

"No one," she called out.

"I wanted to see you so badly," Toribio whispered in tender Spanish. "I've missed you so sorely."

She looked at him, then, whispering herself, said, "*Diez años,* and *now* you want to see me so badly? *Diez años* I wait for you; *tantas cartas te escribo.* But you never write back, hardly call on the *teléfono,* only two or three times. And you missed me?" In the moonlight, her tears glistened. "In ten years, those I loved most, I lost. *Mi madre se murio; mi padre se murio.* I couldn't wait anymore, not knowing nothing, never hearing.

"*Quien es?*" came the man's voice again.

"*Quien es?*" Toribio asked.

Dulce looked at him as if an injured hand and foot were the least of his handicaps. "Can't you *see?*" she asked. "Don't you *hear?* God gave me another chance for marriage. *Un hombre muy bueno,* and he loves me."

Toribio looked at the tile roof of the nice house and at the branches of an apple tree hanging heavily over the masonry fence. They were loaded with fruit.

"I will also have much money now," he said.

"It was not money I waited for."

What Toribio never had to tell her was that he had come back to Julimes not to marry, but to hire her. With the infusion of much of his ten-thousand-dollar injury settlement, his taquito business could, before winter, get a good foothold in the southwest part of Wyoming—Rawlins and Rock Springs and Evanston. But with his injuries, he was going to be hobbled for a while and would need someone willing to pledge what he wasn't.

⟜ ⟜

If not for the egg, Toribio might really have evicted the tenant he called U-Tah. And pulling the shotgun from beneath the driver's seat to expedite the process, he might have said, "No need no sheriff, *tampoco*." It was no stretch to imagine him doing that.

He was already mad, before he banged on the double-wide's door early on the morning of the day before Christmas. Before many months passed, Tate would understand how these infrequent visits just happened to coincide with rent collection, but rent collection was not a priority today. Toribio had been to the pump house, had checked the incubator, had counted: There were no new eggs. And among the old, there were no long-overdue signs of hatching. So far, the brooder lamp had only gathered more dust.

"Why nothing hatch?" was the holiday greeting at the front door. "You keep light turned on in glass always?"

Tate had curtailed a hot shower after a cold jog, only to be met with inquisition by a landlord who, after almost a month away, had chugged into Ashwurm's Last Stand before even going up the road to his own place, wherever that might be. Twice during that month, someone had refilled the feed boxes in the pen, and a well-functioning trough pump had kept the big beaks wet. But there had been no landlord involvement in the husbandry of the birds.

"Don't blame me," Tate said. "The only thing I have to do with those eggs is that incubator burning my juice."

He should have let the matter rest, but when the landlord turned back toward the pump house and fell silent, weighed down no doubt by the image of that barren clutch of blue-green eggs, Tate could not resist salting the wound.

"You ever heard of shell carving and etching?"

While Toribio stared toward the pump house—and, inadvertently, at the flecks of ash around the bomb shelter hole—Tate launched into an explanation, based on something he'd read somewhere, about unviable emu eggs, how they were especially prized in the making of curios, knickknacks, bric-a-brac, that sort of thing. What he didn't know, he admitted, was the status of the local market for decorative eggs or whether it was buyer or seller who took care of sucking out the rotten contents—with a big syringe or whatever, so as to leave just a pinhole. "But," he said, "it might not hurt to ask around. *Comprende?*"

Without blinking, Toribio turned finally and said, "You ve-ry funny guy, U-Tah. *Meester Chistoso.* I no do all this so much for just only knick-knack." Then, as an afterthought, he asked, "What you burn so much?"

Soon thereafter came the discovery of stripped subflooring, then questions and accusations—then, in response, more justifications. Finally, not eager for another stay in Balford Inn, Tate said, "Okay, okay. But before you kick me out, let me at least check for eggs one more time." The truth was, he hadn't been anywhere close to the emu pen in over a week.

Toribio's expression changed immediately—from disgust and distrust to wariness and hope. He really wanted one good egg. After considering for a long moment, he said, "Okay. We check."

All the way out to the pen, past the bomb shelter hole, past the pump house, past the orchard, Tate wondered what he would say when the only thing that would placate the landlord didn't turn up.

Had he considered a vegetarian taquito? If the thing was rolled tight enough, the tofu might not betray itself until the third bite.

From the corner post of the emu pen, they walked one length of fence, then another, searching, peering, scouring. And suddenly, any back-up strategy was moot. In a far corner, the farthest possible distance from a nesting box, lying on a patch of ground aglitter with frost, was the gem of gems. And Tate saw it first. No telling how long it had lain there, exposed to frigid air, yolk and albumen congealing as if in a Popsicle mold. But it was something to point to, which was miracle enough for Tate.

⟹   ⟸

By 11:45, the only people in the Godwin household still awake enough to ring in the new year were Kemp and his guest. They sat in well-worn recliners in the living room. Between the recliners stood a badly scarred coffee table. It held a nearly empty bowl of party mix and two glasses of red punch. A half hour earlier, Kemp's wife had tucked in the only one their six children still at home, a ten-year-old girl, and just before going to bed herself, had come back to say, "Guys, I'm not going to make it."

From time to time, the men looked at the muted television to follow the celebration in Times Square. So far on this cold night, in the three-bedroom house on a quiet street in Balford, Wyoming, drowsiness, not discomfort, had slowed the conversation.

After a long silence, Kemp rubbed his eyes and said, "Didn't I say I'd give you the time off if you wanted to go home for the holidays?"

"Yeah. And I said no thanks. I just got here a month ago."

"What about Santa?"

"There wouldn't have been anything in my stocking anyway. My folks took a Christmas cruise to Hawaii and don't get back till sometime next week."

The questions persisted.

"No other family down there? Nobody else you want to see? It's only—what?—about four hundred miles from here to Spanish Fork?"

"*Five* hundred," Tate said with more shortness than he intended.

Now the lull in their talk was uneasy. They both reached for their glasses and drank punch as if struck simultaneouly with thirst. After replacing his glass on the coffee table, Kemp burped and said, "I'm just asking."

"For a deacon or elder or whatever they call you," Tate said, "you're an okay guy; you really are. But I've told you already: What appealed to me about this gig was the snow. And this is the season to take advantage of that. That's the whole point, right?"

"If you say so."

"First thing Christmas morning I was on the slopes at Sleeping Giant. Took the girl in the lodge all of two minutes to talk me into a season pass and invite me to stay for their party that night. No offense, but their punch had a little more punch to it. It got late, so she let me roll my sleeping bag out in the rent shop. Tuesday through Saturday, ski all day, party all night—now *that's* living."

"What about the egg tending?"

"All taken care of," Tate said. "No *problemo*. All it took was that last one. Once Toribio got it under the heat lamp, he was all smiles, more or less declared the laying season over. He loaded up the incubator—wanted to get it back to his place before anything cooled—knocked half the light bill off my rent, never said another word about the carpet."

"So you're off the hook."

"Hey," Tate said, "he had no right to ask any of that of a tenant in the first place. He's lucky I did what I did."

They fell silent again. The television screen showed images from roving cameras—the brightly lit New Year's ball, skyscrapers, traffic on Manhattan Bridge, the digital count-down clock, the huge crowd in Times Square. For several seconds, one camera focused on a particular young couple, he in a festive red stocking cap, she in a matching ear warmer. They stood close, their breath wreathing each other's faces. They looked happy, content, secure in their affections. When they kissed, the camera lens zoomed in very close.

"But what I can't figure," Kemp mused sleepily, "is why move up *here* for snow? Utah brags about its powder almost as much as Colorado does. Sleeping Giant's okay, but it's no Sundance."

"Ever heard of doing something just for the thrill of it? Or is that against your religion, too?"

"Just for the thrill of it in Balford, Wyoming—now that's some deep and sobering thought, Tate." Kemp Godwin leaned over the arm of his easy chair, scooped a last handful of party mix, then resettled. "I grew up here, and, believe it or not, after a dozen years away—for a mission and school and that first job down in Denver—I actually wanted to come back. It's Podunk, but it's home; anyway, this is where we have *made* our home and will likely keep making it, considering I can see sixty around the corner and am still raising kids."

"The last one was a surprise, huh?"

Kemp looked at his guest. "Not the way you mean it."

"How do you know how I mean it?"

"Like Mormons are pretty hard up for nighttime entertainment; like they're so behind the times they don't know birth control; like who in their right mind would *want* more than two kids. I've heard it all. We can be a pretty self-righteous bunch," Kemp admitted, "but we got no corner on it. What you need to understand is that kid number six in there was a *good* surprise. I wouldn't trade her for the deepest powder on the longest slope in the Alps."

Tate looked at him and said, "It's all what you want out of life, I guess."

"I wanted a mortgage and thirty years warming a swivel chair and a bed with a wife in it," Kemp said. "What about you?"

"What *about* me?"

Kemp had finished his party mix. "I know about the Salt Lake offer, Tate," he said. "You baffled some of the suits when you turned that one down, especially after your uncle ran interference for you with that guy he plays golf with. So you can't blame me for wondering."

Tate spit an ice cube back into his glass and levered down his chair's foot rest. "Look," he said, "I know Mormons, have lived around them all my life. I was hoping to leave the soul-saving in Utah."

"Maybe that's not all you wanted to leave behind."

They looked at each other again as the countdown flashed across the television screen: nineteen, fifteen, ten seconds until the ball dropped in Times Square. Kemp found the television's remote control and turned up the volume just enough to make audible the din of celebration.

"Maybe what I came for and what I left for isn't anything for you to worry about," Tate said.

"No worries," Kemp said drowsily. "Of course not. No worries whatsoever. None."

His eyes closed, and, for several seconds, his breathing lapsed into snoring. Then the snoring stopped, just like that, and the talk resumed:

"We had an old bachelor named Hewell Penroy—didn't get married until his mid-forties. Thing is, he *wanted* it all along, just didn't know where to find a girl, wasn't likely to run into one out in the bean patch. Ended up marrying the meter reader. Then there's Toribio: got all kinds of women, but he wants them with no strings attached. You suppose there's more Hewells or Toribios in the world?"

"I wouldn't know."

At the sound of horns and whistles and cheers, against the spectacle of the milling crowd and fireworks, balloons by the tens of thousands rose into the night sky over New York.

"Just guessing, but I'd say Toribios." Kemp raised his empty punch glass in a toast and said, "Cheers."

〜　〜

When the parents of the Cody Community College sophomore finally got her to disclose Tate's age, they persuaded her—against less resistance than expected—to cancel the Valentine's Day skiing date, which she took care of late Wednesday evening, February 13. Long before sunrise the next morning, since he had already arranged to take the day off, Tate loaded his gear in the back of the Toyota, scraped ice from the windshield, and climbed in the cab. He didn't start the engine. For a long time, he sat staring at the glowing screen of a cell phone with the dimensions of a chocolate bar.

Only a few hours earlier, a cold wind had carried the emu noise away and brought a snatch of salsa across acres of snow-dusted sagebrush. It had to be coming from Toribio's mysterious compound, wherever that was. What was he celebrating with tequila and music? The genius behind taquitos? The crowning hope of his hatching enterprise? The promise of an abundant supply of breast meat and drumsticks? Whatever it was, he surely was doing it in company with one of his women, who would later join him in bed with no strings attached.

Tate had come to Balford committed to selectivity and reserve in answering Brynne's e-mails or text messages, at least until she got over wanting to drag him in to talk with her bishop. But a regular checking of the chocolate-bar screen, from Thanksgiving to Christmas, yielded not a single message on which to exercise that resolution.

Alone at Ashwurm's Last Stand on Christmas eve, after turning down the first of Kemp's invitations to join his family for a holiday meal, when even the barmaid had somewhere else to be, he finally had sent *her* a message, wishing happy holidays and new year—just to let her know he was open to communication.

Three days passed without a response. And such response as there was—*I'm doing fine. Happy new year to you, too*—hardly suggested the pining he had expected. Three weeks later, after the cowgirl from Ralston pulled out a photo of her soldier in Afghanistan, Tate sent another message: *If you ever just want to talk, I'm here.*

The reply this time was immediate: *We had a talk, and it told me everything I needed to know. I think we better both just move on with our lives. I wish you all the best with your plans, whatever they might be.*

She was pressing no claims after all.

At five-thirty on Valentine's morning, it was still very dark. A year ago he had bought roses and chocolates and had taken her, the first time, to Uncle Mont's cabin.

"I wasn't raised to do it this way," she had said afterward, her eyes searching his. "You better be worth it, Tate Rigney."

Sitting in the cold cab of his Toyota, Tate thought of venturing another message. He could tell her how his breath frosting the windshield reminded him of the time they slid off the road on the way to Park City and got rescued by a salt truck. Noting the Toyota's fogged windows, the driver had teased them about what they had been doing to stay warm.

Or he could call. Or, given the occasion, send roses. For old times' sake. Sort of an anniversary. For a moment, the possibility excited him. He started the engine, rolled past the bomb shelter hole and pump house, turned onto McCoullough Road and headed for North Fork and Sleeping Giant. He imagined himself first on the slopes, a lone yellow parka against a vast expanse of knee-deep powder.

"I can't just 'see where it takes us,'" she had said after the third or fourth visit to the cabin. "I need to know this means something to you."

Maybe a call and flowers would be a good move. With or without flowers, maybe such a call would restore things to the way they had been.

He had gone ten miles before it occurred to him that he couldn't have explained what way that was.

⟩ ⟨

On a bright morning in early April, the first time in five weeks, the Suburban turned in at Ashwurm's Last Stand, chugged up to the ditch bordering the orchard and stopped. Three women got out. Lourdes? Giseline? Pilar? Or maybe Mireya and Lupe and Beatriz? One of them raised the glassless hatch, opened the tailgate, and handed out a pair of lopping shears, a bow saw, and leaf rakes. They tied their hair back with scarves and headed into the trees.

Then Toribio hopped out. He turned and reached into the vehicle, then turned back. From the double-wide's living room window, what he held looked like a watermelon with a head growing out of one end.

On this, his fifth month in the double-wide, Tate faced the prospect of the spring thaw with melancholy. The girl at the ski lodge had taken off with some surfer guy from Australia. The seasonal switch of pastimes to golf and maybe windsurfing—if the sport was even known around here—did not excite him as it usually did. But he was curious about that watermelon. He wouldn't wait for the landlord to come collecting. He folded five one-hundred-dollar bills and tucked them in the pocket of his Sleeping Giant T-shirt. Then he jammed his bare feet into hiking boots, and, without lacing them, hurried out the door. He walked fast, boot laces dragging and bouncing down the porch steps and along the ground—past the bomb shelter hole, past the pump house, past the Suburban, across the border ditch and into thick orchard grass, already ankle-high and dripping dew.

In his denim coat and straw hat (still sporting the feather in the band), cradling the watermelon in one arm, Toribio hustled from apple tree to apple tree, from woman to woman. With his back to Tate, he gabbled instructions, pointed with his free hand at branches and limbs and shoots. All three of the laborers were pretty. Even the oldest was twenty-five years younger than the boss, still well within her fertile years. Yet standing only inches from the slope of a slender shoulder, the swell of a blouse, the contour of a shapely backside, he directed his most tender attentions elsewhere. Only when the boss finally turned did Tate see clearly what he held close to his heart.

"Ay, U-Tah," Toribio said, pointing lickety-split to the gangly, watermelon-striped, whisker-headed, pop-eyed fowl. "You see Christmas egg hatch ve-ry good. Already be one month, a little more. You Santa Claus."

Tate stared.

"Emu make ve-ry good meat," Toribio said. "No *grasa*. No cholester-ol. Ve-ry good for grow. I get many eggs more next year."

You see, *gringo baboso, idiota?* He knew what he was doing all along, refusing to give up, even after all those lovely blue-green duds. Ignore the bushels and bushels of feed poured all the long autumn down a dozen feathered gullets for just *one* live embryo; ignore the twisted logic that would make of one hatchling a foundation for a new line of spice-meat for the taquito enterprise. Ignore it all. This was more than vindication; it was true love.

When the shell of this one viable egg finally trembled a week after Valentine's Day, Toribio had been, by coincidence, house-bound with a bad case of the flu. For nearly three weeks, the Suburban enjoyed a rare rest. After broodering snug through the cold of March, first under the rusty cowl of the heat lamp, then by the furnace, then right there at the master's bedside in the mysterious *hacienda,* wherever that was, the bird had become the new hope of his business—and maybe his life.

Handing over the rent money, Tate couldn't help staring at the chick. Already it had outgrown its hatchling cuteness, if it ever could have been called that.

"You save egg ve-ry good," Toribio said in a surprising expression of gratitude. He held the chick out, at arm's length, invited

Tate to take it. The women laughed when, in reflex, Tate's hands shot up like a shield and he back-stepped so fast he tripped. The only other time he had touched a bird, unplucked and unroasted, was on a duck hunt with Brother Delusion and the scouts. After six or eight misses, he had finally blasted a mallard out of the sky over Utah Lake with a longer-barreled version of the same gun that made mincemeat of those feral cats five months back. But that bird was *dead.*

"I bring chick every time in orchard," Toribio promised as he slid the rent money into a hip pocket. "Make ve-ry good mother hen, big and strong. I feed many apples in September. Lot a apples, lot a eggs."

All the way back out of the orchard, with sweet-rotten chunks flattened at every step by his waffle treads, the phrase rang in Tate's head: *Lot a apples, lot a eggs.* What would make the next fall any different? Surely the most recent harvest had been anticipated and noted, yet it now lay moldering into orchard sod. What kind of guy grew with no provision for picking? All those thousands of windfalls and not one pie or fritter to show for them, no cleanly sliced wedges on a fruit tray, no juicy bite to complement the tuna or peanut butter or cold pizza. One entire season's yield, the fruit of Dove Ashwurm's hope and foresight— all left to the weather, to birds and bugs, squandered. When Tate first saw Brynne's mother, she was standing with a paring knife in front of a kitchen sink full of bobbing windfalls. "Waste not, want not," she had said, offering him the one salvageable cut of a wormy gala.

In new grass by the border ditch lay one rare survivor—frost-burned and mushy, but seemingly intact. A hard toe-kick splattered it against the nearest tree trunk. Jarred from unseen holes in the rotten fruit, a dozen chilled beetles took flight.

⇒   ⇐

Breaking with habit in the weeks that followed, through the very end of the skiing season, Toribio stayed close to home, came often to the orchard to irrigate, to scythe new grass and gather ditch-bank asparagus for the penned emus. And always the chick came with him as a companion and showpiece. The bigger it got—too big now for arm cradling—the more it brought out odd paternal impulses in the landlord.

During May's rent collection, all his tenants had to watch the same performance. But Tate, more than the others, was expected to exclaim and applaud the bird's talents.

"Ve-ry fast running, eh?" Toribio said when his dodging and feinting and jinking could not shake the little fellow. He laughed and laughed at the urgent, outstretched neck and beak, the fluffing of feathers, the dogged imprinted allegiance. "Ve-ry *inteligente,* eh?"

He managed to chuckle even when the bird was not so *inteligente.* In a futile attempt at housebreaking, he spread newspaper on his floors, then over and over forgave the bird's knack for finding unpapered spaces.

Through the rest of May, they were inseparable. On every trip out and about, the little emu stood in the middle of the Suburban's front seat, like a sentinel, consigning willing women to the back seat. What went through those women's minds when they saw Toribio pop raisins and peanuts into the little parted beak, stroke the ungainly head, heard him whisper endearments in his native tongue? What did they think, after being so long addressed themselves as only *chica,* when he *named* it?

Plumas de Tortuga.

Turtle Feathers.

➤ ➤

On the first Monday in June, Kemp Godwin stepped across the hall of the little FHA building and handed Tate his mail.

"Danajean saw a letter with real handwriting," he said, making no move toward his own office.

It was from Uncle Mont, a scrawled note on a phone-message pad folded inside a clipping from the wedding section of the *Salt Lake Tribune*:

> *After you fled by night last winter, I played detective, found out her name. Then I saw this the other day. Thought you might like to know.*
>
> *Chin up, Romeo.*

It was an engagement announcement, for Brynne and a guy from Stockton, California. Mormon, of course. He had been a missionary in Russia. It was a good photograph of them both—color, from the Sunday edition, May 26. For a second-year medical student at the U, he looked young. She looked lovely—and happy. They were getting married at her parents' house on the Fourth of July. Her bishop would officiate.

"You okay?" Kemp asked.

Tate handed the clipping to his boss and said, "It wasn't just the snow."

⇒　⇐

For reasons Tate saw more and more clearly, Toribio's affection for the little bird was doomed. The contentment and amusement, the happy interludes at his Balford properties, the companionable comings and goings—none of it could last. Little by little, the bird's instinctive loyalty, so gratifying during the fledgling stage, began to wear on him. With paving and guardrail contracts let, with another busy summer season of taquito vending ahead of him, he could hardly afford to be handcuffed to a bird.

"I no can take it every-*where*, every trip I go," he told Tate a few days after the arrival of Uncle Mont's note. As he lamented unfamiliar obligations, his three-month-old pet, standing dutifully behind him, stretched its neck and began nibbling at a torn belt loop on the Goodwill pants. Through clenched teeth, Toribio said, "*Madre de dios,*" slapped the ugly head away, wheeled and menaced—"*sssssssss!*"—even cocked his tennis shoe for a kick. The emu, stripeless now and not so little, retreated just out of range, remained trusting, eager, unperturbed. Pointing first to the Suburban, then to the bird's well-developed middle toe, the landlord said, "Little *pendejo* poke hole in my ve-ry good front seat." As he spoke, he held up the index finger of his good hand and curved it like a claw.

What finally overtaxed the landlord's forbearance was the mud bath. One evening in the middle of June, after a sudden downpour, the bird wandered away from the orchard and wound up at the bomb shelter hole, where it flirted with the crumbling rim until it managed to fall in. There was nothing for it but to go in after the silly thing. It was bad enough to sink knee-deep into a slurry of ash and mud, and clunk around and around amid charred aluminum cans while the panicked bird squawked and flapped out of reach. But when Toribio finally caught it, the mud-coated feathers painted solid what had been merely spattered. Back on the bank, pressing and wringing cocoa-colored water from his pant legs, the landlord said, "I should maybe let it drown."

The answer to the bird's claim on him was simple—put it in with the flock. As had long since been proven, so long as one of the hired women kept an eye on the feeder boxes and Tate kept electricity flowing to the pump house, the flock could be left for weeks at a time.

The problem was timing: It was still too early for such assimilation. With each visit to Ashwurm's Last Stand, the pet chick ventured closer to the emu pen, curious but timid, until the afternoon it walked right up to the high fence and began pacing. Every few steps, it stopped, cocked its head, and stared. It was only a matter of time before the head found its way through a square in the woven wire. Curious and innocent enough, but a few of the big birds took umbrage, their neck feathers flaring as they rushed toward the visitor. Perceiving the hostility at the last possible moment, the chick just managed to retract its head— but not before one of those pick-handle legs flew high and its middle claw clipped the tip of the little beak.

⇒ ⇐

Shortly after dawn on the Fourth of July, thirty-eight years after Orlin Ashwurm predicted imminent apocalypse, seven or eight hours before Brynne's wedding, the yellow tailgate pulled up to the emu pen and stopped. Even on Toribio's unpredictable schedule, it was early in the day for a visit. Just back from his jog, Tate stood in the orchard next to a pile of prunings and a half-handled leaf rake missing its middle teeth. He was well concealed. The landlord got out—alone. No shabby denim coat, no plumed hat. He was shaved and combed, wore a snap-button western shirt, new jeans, nice cowboy boots. He looked around, then reached under the driver's seat. His hand emerged holding, not a shotgun, but a length of twine.

As Toribio approached the rear of the vehicle, the pet emu's head reached through the glassless window hatch, then turned and inclined as if to nibble a fresh-shaved jaw. Gently, Toribio pushed the beak to one side and, in the same motion, slipped a loop around the long, feathered neck. He raised the hatch, then unlatched the tailgate and let it down. A tug on the twine, a cluck of the tongue, and the bird hopped to the ground, eagerly followed the boss along the high fence, toward the corner gate.

At the gate, Toribio tucked the lead-twine under one arm and, despite the use of nine sound fingers, took a long time with the cobbled wire fastenings. Eventually the gate swung open, just wide enough for him and the bird. Five feet inside the pen, and cautious of where he stepped in such nice boots, he stopped. He unsnapped one of the shirt's pockets, fished out something—fig? prune? cherry tomato?—and popped it into the open beak.

He undid the rope. Again and again he stroked the feathers on the long neck and domed turtle back. Then, placing the palm of the maimed hand alongside the whiskered head, he leaned and kissed his pet just above the beak.

Tate was witness to it all.

And that was it. Toribio stepped back through the gate and fastened it. He looked once toward the little bird, hesitated, then, in his forward-leaning way, hustled faster than ever toward the Suburban. Without breaking stride, he got to the cab and hopped in. As on a thousand other occasions, he was in a hurry to be gone.

Freedom, man—it gets in your blood.

That was the postscript on the back side of Uncle Mont's note.

Chug-chug-chug. Tate watched the yellow tailgate into the sunrise and out of sight. *Adiós*, Toribio. Then he turned to the pen. It hadn't taken long for the rest of the flock to realize what was standing in the corner by the water trough, unmoved from where Toribio had made his farewell—on *their* side of the fence. By then, of course, Toribio was well down McCoullough Road, headed, as it happened, to Billings, to pick up a commercial roaster one of his many women had bought at a liquidation auction the week before. Ve-ry good for cooking spice-meat.

So the boss didn't have to see the big birds distracted from their morsel-pecking, drawn toward that particular corner of their pen, quickening their pace, neck feathers just beginning to flare. Nor did he have to hear those three-pronged feet scuffing along the floor of their enclosure as they circled the newcomer. Or the hissing beaks. Or the woven wire vibration when the first claw barely missed.

But Tate did. In the time it took to grab the gap-toothed leaf rake and cover the distance to the pen at a hard run, at least half a dozen birds improved on the aim of the first one. It was that sudden.

"He-ey!" Tate yelled. "HEY!"

Forced from its corner, the little emu limped in a daze and was struck again, twice. In no time, it was down, surrounded by a species of fowl known for extraordinarily strong leg muscles. Meanwhile, Tate fumbled at the same wire fastening, flung open the same gate, rushed the mob with the rake held high.

"Hey-hey-hey! Get away from there! HEY-EEY!"

But he was too late. The reluctant dispersing of the circle revealed the effects of the welcome—two trembling twig legs, blood-matted feathers, gaping beak, marble eyes dumb with amazement. Not five minutes after the Suburban's departure, Toribio's pet was as good as dead. That was the only tenable verdict, arrived at as Tate crouched and stared. At some point in his stupor, he heard, behind him, a vague rushing sound and, again too late, perceived it for what it was—the air-stir of fluffed plumage. Just as he rose and turned, he heard the hiss of the biggest hen in the flock, saw, in the same instant, the long neck stiffened like a flagpole, the dark eyes, the open beak, the out-lashing of a middle toe. If not for a lucky, stumbling dodge, the toe-claw would have drilled his thigh like a railroad spike. As it was, the contact came at the extreme of the claw's downward arc and just poked him. Which was bad enough.

Tate could never decide on the greater motivation—the chick's fate or his own—for trying to behead the attacker with the leaf rake. Either way, he came gratifyingly close. Despite being off-balance and shaky with adrenalin, he managed a fairway swing, caught the head broadside, bloodied the hen's upper neck and the side of her face pretty nicely; when she backed off, she was wincing, weaving the whiskered skull as if responding to a snake charmer. He had never wished for anything as he now wished for Toribio's shotgun.

Tate got to the trough and flushed the wound. It wasn't all that deep, but had already bled down his leg and soaked the elastic band of his sock. Mid-summer or not, the trough water was cold enough to raise goose bumps. The bruising hurt worse than the puncture, but even a speck of feces could infect your blood. He remembered that fact from first aid training in scouts. He took off the jogging tank top and made a bandage of it, the way Brother Delusion had showed them.

Gradually the morsel-pecking resumed. When Tate knelt beside the little bird, his thigh knotted, and, for just an instant, his head swam. The bird was barely breathing. Forking both arms under the body, he stood. With the limp legs and flopping neck, the burden was unwieldy. With the bloody feathers, it was a mess. As Tate bore the bird through the gate and along the fence, its weight kept rolling and shifting, and its lungs made a purring noise. By the time he reached the orchard, the purring had stopped. It was dead.

Nothing was raised to end up this way.

Orlin Ashwurm never would have imagined such uses for his bomb shelter hole—garbage dump, burn pit, and, thirty-eight years after its digging, a grave. After Tate had laid the little bird in the floor of the hole, which was still slimy several weeks after the mud bath, he climbed out and stood looking down at it for a long time. Then he grabbed the same shovel that had cleaned up what was left of the feral cats and, with a thrust and a fling, started backfilling. Over toward Willwood a few fireworks went off. Firecrackers—*pa-pop, pa-pop, pa-pop*—then the scream of a bottle rocket. Some kid, impatient for the darkness.

"You got a heart, a head, and hormones," Brother Delusion said during one of his frequent campfire devotionals. "The trick in life is a righteous balance of the three."

At last the pile was leveled, the hole filled, the burial finished.

Have you considered your options?

What was hurting was the bruise. The poke wasn't so bad. Douse it with rubbing alcohol, duct-tape a folded washcloth over it, and go discover at long last where Toribio Gomez lived his private life.

Follow the gray gravel road.

Its washboard ridges jarred wheel alignment and a throbbing thigh. But it took him where he had to go, as far as the NO

TRESPASSING—PRIVATE PROPERTY sign hung crookedly on the padlocked metal gate.

Leave the truck and climb, quite nimbly, up and over that gate. Even so—painful. That bruise was like a canker, made every step a charley horse.

Follow the track bulldozed through sagebrush seven feet tall. It crowded the narrow track so closely it must have scraped the Suburban's sides at every pass. And its shade was no shade at all. Not yet mid-morning, and already the big silver boughs radiated heat.

Follow the curved and rough-bladed swath for at least a third of a mile, through two barbed-wire gates. The sore thigh forced a stiff limp under a glare growing brighter by the minute. Finally, finally, come to the six-foot chainlink enclosing the compound itself—topped with three more strands of barbed wire—and the gate into the heart of the place.

Somewhere in the foothills around Mt. Nebo, just south of Spanish Fork, one of their hikes had taken the scouts past an abandoned sawmill enclosed with a chainlink fence. PRIVATE PROPERTY—NO TRESPASSING. Securing the gate was a light-gauge chain and a padlock that hadn't known a key for a very long time. A year or two later, several of those uninterested in merit badges went back—with different companions and no Brother Delusion to supervise. They took bolt cutters that time, thought it chivalrous not to ask girls to find narrow toeholds on hinges or straddle barbed wire six feet in the air. Yet they saw no incongruity in asking those same girls to drink warm beer from cans and relax the most profound of restraints in piles of sawdust fifty years old. All the way back to Spanish Fork, it clung to clothing, especially underwear.

Follow the hardpan driveway.

Past Toribio's chainlink gate and just beyond a windbreak of Russian olives, the full fruits of rich-*dueño* ambition came into view.

The drive divided a big garden plot. Who would come to weed and water the peppers for the spice-meat? Caridad? Elsa? Josefina?

And finally, finally, there was the *hacienda,* walled with unpainted cinder block, roofed with corrugated metal. Like a jailhouse. Every window stood caged behind a grill of welded rebar, and the thick front door featured a six-inch galvanized hasp and padlock to match. This was where he stayed when he stayed anywhere at all, where he incubated the egg, broodered the chick, now and again brought a hopeful, trusting woman who wished they would do what they did with more promise of permanence.

The morning was hot and still. Next to the house stood a shed. Under its awning sat an old golf cart. What a strange relief to find no clubs anywhere close, no shared interest in the game. The little cargo box held only a rusty roofing hatchet, pair of fencing pliers, can of staples. Off toward the river, maybe a hundred yards distant, lay the goat pasture sloping toward a stand of willows. The gate in the pasture fence was never closed after the discovery of the coyote plundering.

Somehow Brother Delusion found out about the party at the abandoned sawmill. That was the only time Tate ever saw him angry: "All I've ever tried to do is teach you to become decent men, and you go and pull a crap-stunt like that."

The beer and chain-cutting bothered him, but not a fraction as much as the other.

"How could you *do* that to young women?" he asked. "They deserve better."

Follow the golf cart path.

A hot breeze had come up. Nothwithstanding the bruised thigh, follow in curiosity, to the acreage behind the house. Maybe it was a backyard wedding. White gown and green grass and flowers in profusion. Tiered cake thick with frosting. Mixed nuts. Butter mints. Punch with no punch. The bishop in his gray suit. Her parents happy for a reliable man at long last, a man with some direction, a man ready to try to be what a woman deserved. Church people would witness the union, wait to wish the couple well, then dig into the finger sandwiches and little cups of potato salad and the fruit tray edged with unblemished apple wedges. And tonight she would be the medical student's wife, in a proper bed, with no mice in the mattress.

In the distance, more firecrackers, another bottle rocket.

It was several days before even the most irreverent of the sawmill partiers tried to laugh off Brother Delozier's reprimand. More hair in his nostrils and ears than on his scalp. A shiny film of saliva between his lips whenever he got emotional during his admonitions and exhortations. But the quavering voice and teary eyes were not so easily mocked after all.

Follow the faintest, final trail.

And come at last to a world of animal accommodations—pens and shelters, runs and brooder huts, row upon row of hutches, coops, cages. Chinchillas, Cornish hens, Guinea fowl, Minzhu pigs. Meandering aisles, walkways, frontage. Water and scratch troughs, hair snagged on nail heads, relic litter, pits and rinds from a bygone swill bucket, scattered feathers. Everything vacant and abandoned.

In a sudden hot gust, a hinge squeaked. Tate wheeled in a panic, searching the sky for great turtle wings. But except for an approaching dustdevil, the sky, too, was empty. Alone, eyes wide open, he stood before the gritty swirl and heard in its wind a medley of bleating and cooing and clucking.

CHARIOT RACE IN D-WING

IT WAS THOSE TWO WHEELCHAIRS IN THAT NURSING home in Billings last week that got me thinking again about the movie. *Ben-Hur* and I go way back. April 4, 1960. It was a Monday night. I remember because it was my eighth birthday, the age of accountability, according to Mormon doctrine. Given the occasion, I was allowed to eat my second saucer of cake and ice cream in front of our little black and white TV. Given where we lived—up toward Heart Mountain, halfway between Balford and Cody—our antenna picked up only one station. But that one station happened to be showing the Academy Awards ceremony. It was soon clear that Mr. Wyler's screen adaptation of Mr. Wallace's book was the darling of the evening.

"That must be some movie," said my dad, who had worked all day flushing and rehanging a basement sewer line, a job the plumber before him had cut a lot of corners on.

Just before Bob Hope (the program's host) announced the movie's unprecedented eleventh and final award, my mother came into the living room, wet to the elbow from washing the dishes of my birthday meal, and told me to go to bed. She said she didn't want me yawning through my own baptismal service the next evening. Then she placed a warm-wet hand on my head and asked, by way of preparatory quiz, "And what is it you commit to when you go down in the water?"

"To always remember Jesus and keep his commandments," I recited, straight from our sacrament prayers.

"And?" she prompted, fishing for an addendum of her own.

"To love and forgive others."

⇒   ⇐

When I met Norris Grubgeld, I was twenty-seven and had watched *Ben-Hur* almost every Easter since my eighth birthday. In that time, I had come to greatly admire its theme, an addendum to my mother's addendum: *how* to forgive, when such seems beyond human capacity. This, of course, is one of the grand tenets of Christianity. Thanks to a thousand sermons and Sunday school lessons, I knew it as well as I knew the sacrament prayers. It is a tenet I believe in, the only thing that explains why some wronged souls find peace and others don't. As a bishop, the lay leader of the little ward in Balford, I regularly recommend it one on one to people who, for one reason or another, are not at peace. Yet it's clear to me now that admiring and recommending were all the farther I, Bishop Ed Beverly, had gone with that theme—until I happened into Grubgeld last week in Golden Oaks Nursing Home in Billings, Montana.

A long-unaddressed grudge and its eventual remedy make the only defensible parallel between my story and the movie's story. For starters, Grubgeld was not a boyhood friend, as the Roman military tribune Messala is to Judah Ben-Hur; his power was exerted, not over the Jews in first-century Jerusalem, as Messala's is, but over five English teachers, a speech instructor, and a libidinous drama coach at a place called Gafton College on the plains of Nebraska; and he never asked me to betray my people.

But he did fire me. He was the only boss in my life who saw fit to do that. You are now one of humanity's wronged souls, Ed Beverly! In the twenty-five years since the firing, I had actually gotten to the point where I could laugh at such self-pitying rubbish. But time is responsible for that progress; time takes the edge off almost everything. And self-mockery is not forgiveness, which I realized very clearly when the mere sound of elbow crutches somewhere down a hall in the D-Wing of that nursing home (*D* for dementia) triggered exactly the same chill it triggered twenty-five years earlier.

Nothing notable about crutches in such a place except I *knew* this pair. The *ca-chunk* of wrist-collar linkage put me right back in that basement hall of the humanities building at Gafton College. When I had last seen Grubgeld, two states away, on an evening in mid-May of 1982, *he* was fifty-five, as I now am, and putting on his doctoral regalia for that year's commencement exercises. I had stepped into the hall for a drink at the water fountain and caught a glimpse of him, from behind, settling his cap onto his ears, which, by virtue of their size and flare, would prevent it from settling any farther. By long tradition, commencement was held in the Oscar P. Duworth Chapel, on the other side of the tidy little Presbyterian campus, and, considering his means of mobility, he was going to have to hurry.

We were the only two still on the hall. Exempted as I was from attending graduation, I was using the time to box my things so as to meet the unsigned vacancy deadline (by sundown or else!) mysteriously taped to my office door during the hour I was gone for lunch. Exemption from graduation, by the way, was granted only for the direst of circumstances and required the approval of not only Chairman Grubgeld, but of his boss as well, a bow-tied, pipe-smoking dean by the name of Artie Lemon. By five, my colleagues were gone. The last three out were my friend Isaac Freed, workaholic Mildred Jo Fitzmeyer, and Hearn the libidinous drama coach (accompanied by two female students willing to laugh at enough of his suggestive jokes to secure an *A* in their "Stage Methods" class). It was an ideal moment for a farewell from the boss, yet there was no farewell. Grubgeld did not come up the hall to me, nor, in fairness, did I walk down the hall to him. All the best, Ed. Same to you, Nate. What would it have hurt either of us to say such words, to say *something*?

⇒   ⇐

Shortly into its three-and-a-half hours, *Ben-Hur* becomes a story of grievance. When Judah refuses to disclose and help stamp out every last pocket of Jewish rebellion, Messala contrives to condemn his mother and sister to a leprous dungeon and Judah himself to an oar bench in one of Caesar's galleys. Off-camera, for good measure, Messala orders the torture and imprisonment of Simonides, faithful servant to the House of Hur and father of Judah's love interest, Esther.

I am well acquainted with other people's grievances, little and big. You can't teach as long as I've taught (Gafton plus Cody Community makes twenty-eight years) without hearing every student lamentation under the sun. And halfway through a projected six years or so as a Mormon bishop, I spend a lot of time listening to hard accounts of sickness, financial trouble, addiction, wayward-ness, selfishness, sexual folly. It is a rare case that doesn't involve one human wronging another. Some of the hurt in those accounts settles so heavily on me that leaving the bishop's office late Sunday or on a mid-week evening is like trudging a sand pit.

Still, I don't *personally* know grievance as Judah knows griev-ance. By comparison, being fired is small-fry. For that matter, I don't know grievance as Grubgeld knows it. Neither polio nor accident accounts for his paraplegia. I heard the story from Isaac Freed. At the bedside of eight-year-old Norrie Grubgeld, the doc-tor attributed the belly ache to gas, a diagnosis that greatly relieved parents who had to make do from the collection plate of a tiny Presbyterian church in my boss's hometown of Burr, Nebraska. By the time the screams forced a midnight trip to a hospital forty miles away in Lincoln—half that distance by dirt road—the appen-dix had already ruptured. Oddly, the infection spared the organs and settled in the lower part of the spinal cord. Two weeks after the surgery, young Norrie crawled clumsily out of his hospital bed only to realize that, notwithstanding the doctor's assurances, movement did *not* restore the feeling in his toes and legs. Specialists in Omaha confirmed that the handicap was permanent.

Freed first heard that story from senior department member Phyllis Lundquist, who had heard it directly from Grubgeld, shortly after his arrival at Gafton, in 1955, two years after her own. Despite her seniority, despite competence and leadership potential quite a bit more promising than his, she was passed over for chair. Phyllis had a nose for humbug, which understandably put a man like Artie Lemon on constant guard, no matter how studiously he affected calm with the smoking of his pipe. Hence the perceived thwarting when, instead of winning the chair position—to which she was unquestionably entitled but in which she would have been uncomfortably close to some of Gafton's richest veins of humbug—she found herself sitting on yet another committee. *What would we ever do without you, Phyllis?* She remembered, at the end of the appendix story, Grubgeld's lip trembling and his voice so choked he could hardly finish his last sentence— much like her own lip and voice when she recounted her long history at Gafton College.

That kind of grievance—the faulty diagnosis, the parental oversight, the job snub, the genteel exploitation—puts mine in its place. But, big or little, it was the grievance that was mine to deal with. On an afternoon in mid-March of 1982, Grubgeld approached my not quite fully closed office door (stealth was not one of his gifts) and said, "Knock-knock-knock." Before I could even respond, the big rubber floor grip of one crutch snaked between door and jamb, and more or less flung aside the one sure barrier between him and me. "Got a minute?" he said, more as a command than a question.

According to a practice by then familiar to me, reprimands took place in *his* office. So what was this? He maneuvered, stifflegged, to the ratty visitor's chair, leaned his crutches against my bookcase, then dropped into the seat like a sandbag. "Ed," he said, after shifting and settling, "I hate that it's come to this, but you haven't left me a lot of choice. Dean Lemon is right about that."

Despite the gravity of the moment, there was a certain rueful humor to the claim that a man like Artie Lemon was right about *anything*. Rueful humor unabashed was my dad's reaction when I showed up back in Balford, tail between my legs. He could hardly regard the loss of that particular job as much of a blow. "Six years of college," he said, "and you could've made more unplugging toilets." My dad had waded ashore at Tarawa amid floating limbs and torsos and thus knew more at age eighteen about indignity and injustice than I ever will. When the war ended, he came home to a trade that required dealing, at all hours, with pipes full of unspeakable nastiness. Compared to what *could* come from such experience, rueful humor looks pretty good.

Don't misunderstand me. Whatever equanimity I might have claimed before my recent visit to Golden Oaks Nursing Home took twenty-five years to accrue—after a very slow start. On the actual occasion of my firing, my dander was up, hackles raised, spleen well exercised—in response to both the bad news and to the man delivering it. We had never liked each other. It was only with misgivings that he offered me a job in the first place and only out of desperation that I took it.

"And this religion of yours," he had said toward the end of the job interview, "you have no plans to bring it into the classroom, I trust?"

It took only the first reprimand for me, the new hire with the oddball BYU on his transcript (instead of the typical U of N or Bellevue or Chadron), to know the dangers of "bringing" my religion anywhere Grubgeld might catch a whiff of it. Early in my first semester, after handing out copies of a short story by a Mormon writer—to supplement an anthology unit featuring Catholic writers and Protestant writers and Jewish writers—I was summoned to his office.

"Ed," he said, "I thought I made myself more than clear on this sort of thing."

The offense, I gathered, was a mixing of church and school. Never mind that Mildred Jo Fitzmeyer, in her technical writing class, taught the rudiments of document layout by having her students assemble the weekly bulletin for Gafton First Methodist's Sunday service. Or that cheerful Tatum, speech teacher and part-time Baptist youth minister, used Bible-camp songs (accompanied by his guitar) to help students overcome stage fright. Or that Hearn the libidinous drama coach could, for twenty years, bring *his* religion of randy innuendo into classrooms and rehearsals, could regularly lubricate that innuendo with Beefeater's gin, and so long as Gafton's little auditorium filled on opening night, there was never a censure.

I didn't realize the *specific* complaint against me and my religion until the second year's reprimand. In a lesson on the amazing human capacity for taxonomy, I had listed on the chalkboard as many religions and subdivisions of religions as the students could think of. It was foolish enough to add mine to the list at all, but the death knell was locating it under the Christian heading. The Church's full name, as I explained (while incriminating myself with chalk left unerased), is the Church of *Jesus Christ* of Latter-day Saints. Yes, I granted, it's a mouthful, but it serves as solid verification for those who are suspicious of the focus of our worship.

Like Grubgeld.

"Ed," he said, after another summons to his office, "we are a progressive school, but we also have to be mindful of our heritage. We are, after all, a Christian college and are understandably discomfited by cults."

"Mormonism isn't a cult," I said. In response to his dry chuckle and skeptical smile, I said—bravely, proudly, insubordinately, "I'm just as Christian as you are."

For twenty-five years I have pondered the several ironies of that declaration.

After that reprimand, accompanied by a mandatory "Personal Improvement Plan" (*PIP*), I could have shined his orthopedic shoes, made his coffee, brought him baked goods every morning—as young colleague Libby McBride did—and never, in the remainder of his career, won his favor. At least that's what I tell myself. We had never been easy in one another's company, but after my Christianity boast, everything became adversarial.

Pick your example: During each of my three Decembers at Gafton, I left for Christmas break, and for Balford, *before* the department get-together at his house. Number two: I did not devise multiple-choice and true-false exams to mathematically counter poor grades on actual writing assignments. (*Artie Lemon is the walking embodiment of the Peter Principle—T or F.*) Alas, to mark those assignments, I used pencil and not department-issue red pens. Number three or four or whatever: I showed up for work each day earlier than the boss, which upset his routine considerably. Now *I* unlocked the main door and flipped on the hall light; now *I* got the first cold swallow of the day from the freshly disinfected water cooler; now *I* went first into the shiny-clean bathroom before settling into a swivel chair to note all other arrivals, including his. And I did most of that noting by ear since my door was almost fully closed, its hinge angle nowhere near the strongly suggested ninety degrees.

"Ed," he said in one of many moments of exhortation, "a fully open door sends a better message to our students." (This from a man whose antipathy for students was topped only by his antipathy for problem faculty members.)

Trifling and ludicrous as they were, such points became the substance of a constant antagonism. Considering his nature and considering mine—frequently *un*Christian, both of them—it was only a matter of time before I gave him grounds to fire me. Obviously he wanted a reason that wouldn't *seem* to have anything to do with my religion. Yet there really could be no such reason for me. In saying that, I am not claiming persecution; I mean that if I had *practiced* the religion I profess, if I had heeded my mother's addendum, I could have negotiated the frictions and kept my job. Mormonism is generally known for its prohibitions—tobacco, alcohol, illicit sex, and so on. But compared to loving your enemy, chastity is a cakewalk.

Eventually, as I said, Grubgeld found his reason to have done with me. As it happened, I was not enthusiastic about his favored method of marginally annotating student essays. This method, imported from some bygone conference workshop, was known in Gafton's humanities department as *RCS*. *Review-Consult-Solidify!* Cryptic annotations, coded to sections of a grammar handbook, were drilled by the hour in mandatory department "in-service" sessions—as if just the right abbreviation, located beside a line containing this or that error, would somehow transform already certified carelessness into a sudden eagerness to correct and master. Pedagogically, the method was pure delusion. But pedagogy, I finally realized, wasn't the point; the point was window dressing to persuade Dean Artie Lemon we were earning our keep. Yet there must have been a better way of communicating my regard for RCS than the way I chose in a department meeting in January of my third and final year. The whole approach, I argued, was Ridiculous-Comical-Stupid! And in saying so, I was Rude-Captious-Strident!

The truth is, RCS was no more delusional than most education quackery. Quackery is the coin of the realm and will forever have to be conceded by anyone who wants to teach. That fact wasn't Grubgeld's fault. Like me, like all of us, he had to live with contradictions and absurdities over which he had no control. Over time, that sort of impotence becomes a grievance all its own. Had I worried less about my defiance, I could have better seen the reasons for his.

And who could begrudge the man some defiance? A lifetime of rough terrain, starting with schoolyard miseries unnumbered, had brought him, by the time of our acquaintance, to some tried-and-true survival strategies: a felt businessman's hat to protect his balding scalp, dark sun lenses clipped onto earthquake-resistant eyeglass frames, suspenders of sturdy elasticity, and different sole thicknesses on his cobbler-custom shoes to level his world as much as it could be leveled. And he was scrupulously independent. Though the college offered the use of its golf cart, he made a point of getting to questionably distant campus locations, like Duworth Chapel, under his own power. And he *always* carried his own things—briefcase, lunch box, umbrella—even made a point of not allowing others to open doors for him. "I've got it, thanks," he said over and over, everywhere, all the time, all his life, until the curtness was as reflexive as breathing.

Grubgeld's handicap, coincidentally, is the same handicap Simonides is left with after being tortured in a Roman dungeon called The Citadel. After his release, he owes his mobility to an ox of a man named Malluch, a fellow inmate left mute by his torturers. "Since then," Simonides explains to Judah, "I have been his tongue, and he has been my legs. Together we make a considerable man." As far as I know, Grubgeld has had no Malluch in his life, has allowed no such alliance with another human being.

After enough years away from Gafton, I came to pity Grubgeld. But my pity was more dodge than compassion. Pity of that kind I could give the man because pity is easy. It yields self-approval without any change of heart. And change of heart is what any Christian religion, especially mine, should be about. I lost my job not because I was Mormon, but because I wasn't Mormon enough.

⇒   ⇐

Given the nature of grievance, it's only logical that *Ben-Hur* is also a story of revenge. "Your eyes are full of hate," says Quintus Arrius when, as the new fleet consul, he first confronts Judah on an oar bench in the bowels of a galley. "That's good. Hate keeps a man alive; it gives him strength." What Arrius can't know is the object of that hate. Caesar Tiberius? The swarthy drummer who marks the rowing cadence? The calluses on the hands and rump of a nobleman? Maybe, in some perverse way, Arrius sees the hate of the galley slaves as a tribute to his own over-seer beneficence. "We keep you alive to serve this ship," he says upon assuming command of this particular vessel. "So row well and live."

Despite the hackles raised by the boss sitting knee to knee with me in my cramped office, I knew the verdict being deliv-ered had originated in the much more spacious office of Dean Artie Lemon, a world away in the administration building. That verdict was, of course, gravely pondered, piously regretted, then duly documented on a "Personnel Status Form."

"You'll want to take care of this as soon as possible, Nate."

As men go, Artie Lemon and Norris Grubgeld were not par-ticularly bad sorts, no more self-interested than most. Undoubt-edly they regarded the firing as an unsavory chore that came with the territory. But what if the *territory* is the grievance? The machinations of systems and institutions, underlings stacked on more underlings, bureaucracy thick as backfat—show me any part of life that doesn't take you into such territory. It's hard to put a face on that.

But in the end the object doesn't much matter. Bitterness is bitterness, and it's not the object it cankers. This truth is well evident to the movie's wise-man character, Balthasar. Not very far into his first meeting with Judah, he sorrows over the same quality Arrius commends: "I see this terrible thing in your eyes, Judah Ben-Hur." On the matter of hatred, Esther would side with the wise man. "Blood gets more blood," she tells Judah, "as dog begets dog."

After I was fired, the closest I came to craving vengeance was the indulging of a fantasy. This period of indulgence was brief,

and the fantasy itself, pretty bland. In it, I always found my Gafton bosses in some unlikely predicament—waterless in Death
Valley, blanketless in the Arctic, ladderless in a pit. The important point in my fantasy was that *I* had the upper hand:

We keep you alive to serve this college, so row well and live.

No sooner had Grubgeld told me my days were numbered
than he said, "I want you to know, Ed, this is not personal."
Though popular as a rationalization, that line is tripe. Even if, in
the matter of my firing, it were true of my boss—and it wasn't—
it certainly wasn't true of me. In any firing, there's always a *person* who soon won't have a job to go to Monday morning or a
paycheck to pick up on Friday. To the aggrieved, grievance is
always personal! Without that fact, Judah would have no story.
More to the point, *I* would have no story.

Regarding the *actual* fates of my Gafton bosses, I cannot be so
cavalier as I was in fantasy. Among the news in a surprise phone
call from Isaac Freed, some years back, was passing mention of
Artie Lemon's death from lung cancer. After all those committee meetings and council meetings and cabinet meetings, the
perennial convulsions over enrollment, retention, accreditation,
all that sloganeering and acronymic gobbledygook—after all
that, Dean Artie Lemon finally made it to the coveted pinnacle
from which golf greens and pension checks stretch to the horizon. But not a month after the retirement reception meatballs
and vegetable tray in the foyer of Duworth Chapel, he woke up
one morning coughing a cough that scared his wife. "Artie, you
are going to *have* to give up that pipe."

And as to Norris Grubgeld, desert and ice floe have nothing
over exile in the D-Wing.

Even if I were to call the fates of these two men poetic justice, such justice would affect me the same way it affects Judah
when Messala's ruthlessness on Judea's chariot track finally back-
fires. "I see no enemy," Judah says to the trampled and dying

tribune. Is he blind? Messala wonders. Or is he not man enough to acknowledge before him, on the surgeon's table, "the smashed body of a wretched animal"? But Judah sees something other than enemy or animal. If not for that one troublesome point, his vengeance would be, as the gasping Messala puts it, a "triumph complete," and the story could end. But Messala's death avenges nothing! It resolves nothing! Judah's mother and sister are still lepers, and more to the point, Judah's bitterness is not in any way assuaged.

Telling the story of grievance is a paradox. The closer the teller comes to rendering his grievance accurately, the more he dooms the story to incompletion. What we actually want, in our resolutions, is a kind of poetic *in*justice: In our hearts we hope for a ladder out of the pit, even when the digging of it is our own doing. That's why the movie can't end with Judah's revenge. In the movie, as in life, there's more to it than that.

〓　〓

The spring of 1982 was a long time ago. I survived, and life worked out. Who knows, for instance, if I ever would have found a wife in Gafton, Nebraska—as I did not too long after moving back to Balford? Vivian Sebright, only child of Darl and Avis. This was not the only time in my life a reversal was compensated. Thanks to a government paperwork glitch, I was denied a missionary deferral and got drafted in July of 1970, my first summer out of high school. We were given to understand that we would be in Vietnam by Christmas. On the foggy December morning our C-130 transport was waiting on the tarmac at Travis Air Force Base, a lieutenant colonel showed up out of the blue, and said, "I don't suppose any of you inbred derelicts know how to type." Thanks to Miss Waterstradt's tenth-grade "Office Methods" class, which my mother had to beg me to take, I spent the rest of my hitch clerking stateside.

Yet somehow it's easier to acknowledge a compensation when the reversal is a vagary, part of the faceless territory of life I was talking about. But suppose there *is* a face behind the reversal. You can acknowledge any number of related mercies, as I have, and still not forgive the face. Letting go of most grievance takes more than a counting of blessings or looking on the bright side or accentuating the positive. All that can't hurt, but it's not the same as making peace. "I've heard of a young rabbi," Esther tells Judah. As she describes it, the young rabbi's voice "traveled with such a still purpose it was more than a voice." And what that voice-more-than-a-voice says, then and now, is that the only way to make peace is to forgive trespasses and love enemies.

Impossible. When finally forced to test such sentiments myself, that's what *I* said. Living such sentiments would take a miracle, and a miracle of that kind always sounds more agreeable—and easier—in Sunday school than it turns out to be Monday morning. After so long in the galleys, Judah claims not to believe in miracles at all. "I must deal with Messala in my own way," he tells Sheik Ilderim. For someone who doesn't believe in God, such a statement is understandable. But from Judah? Irony begets irony. Just before the chariot race, he asks God to forgive *him* for seeking vengeance. That seems a strange and contradictory petition, much like many of my own. Then he ends the prayer by saying, "Into your hands I commit my life." As long as he's asking for contradictions, as long as he's pledging his life, why not ask for and pledge the wherewithal to forgive the unforgiveable?

⇒ ⇐

Initially, my visit to Golden Oaks Nursing Home had nothing to do with forgiveness. Out of duty, and little more, I had come to see the ninety-two-year-old bedridden mother of a disaffected member of the Balford Ward. But I was too late.

"Not more than twenty minutes ago," the receptionist said. "Are you clergy?"

"Sort of," I said.

"She ate such a good lunch," said a girl in floral scrubs. "Even finished all her mashed potatoes."

"I can't call the funeral home until I get a hold of her next of kin," the receptionist said. She kept nervously lifting, then replacing, the telephone receiver in its cradle. "Do you know it's been two weeks since I heard *anything* from that poor lady's family?"

It was the next of kin—the sixty-year-old disaffected daughter—who had called my number at Cody Community College the day before to air a few grievances of her own, chief among them *my* neglect of her mother, a lady who had never lived in Balford, a lady I had never met or, before that phone call, heard of. The deeper enmity, I gathered as the daughter went on and on, was between her and her mother. The scattered details came to this: Some years earlier they had had a falling out, and now, as people do, the daughter was grieving her own grievance.

"I'm sorry you drove all that way," the receptionist said.

No regrets. While in the city, I would do a little shopping, run a few errands, get a bite to eat. I thanked her and turned to leave.

"You just never know when it's your time," said the girl in scrubs, utterly without guile or glibness. "I guess just try to be ready is all you can do."

I had taken several steps, but now stopped. It was as if I had just heard the most profound sermon of my life. If only the disaffected daughter could have heard it in time. Errands and a bite to eat! The smallness of my concerns took my breath away.

And that is when I heard, or *thought* I heard, elbow crutches, somewhere down the D-Wing.

Ca-chunk.

But that wing lay beyond thick double doors. A fire alarm buzzer would hardly have penetrated, let alone the sound of aluminum linkage. How had I heard anything at all? Yet I had. I hesitated, then turned back to the reception desk. It was a peculiar request, but at this point there was nothing for it: I had to venture into that region of the building.

"You *know* someone down there?" the receptionist asked.

There was no explaining the real draw, so I said I tried to visit such places, such people, whenever possible—which, given my church duties, is not entirely untrue.

The receptionist shrugged, said, "I imagine you know what you're in for, then."

I didn't. But I couldn't leave without tracing the sound. I can't explain it. I was curious, anxious, guilty, haunted. And, as I moved toward the D-Wing, I was fixated on the wisdom of the girl in scrubs. Just before one of the thick doors latched behind me—and locked from the lobby side—she called out: "It's like for some of them down there life is frozen seventy years ago."

She was right again. Walking the hall of any D-Wing, anywhere, is like walking through a time tunnel. Most of the residents live in a past only they can see. But, in those residents, most visitors see only too clearly their own futures and, for that reason, are eager to be gone from the place before they even cross the threshold. The impulse is to give a wide berth to the paramedics' draped gurney, ignore the hearse backed up discreetly to a side door, blot out the mattress stripped of its sheets and leak pad, the mop bucket, the cart full of disinfectant bottles, and find the main exit as briskly as your legs will carry you.

Down the well-buffed hall, door by door, room by room, I checked name cards—simple laser-printed 3x5's. Each card fit into a plastic bracket screwed chest-high to the wall beside the door. Hospital, hotel, prison—all in one facility. The din of game shows and soap operas on two dozen wall-mounted televisions didn't *quite* mask the moaning of the bedfast, the mumbling of roamers, the clearly enunciated ramblings of one who stopped me to ask if I was going to the wedding, and another, who needed directions to a movie theater in Santa Fe.

"You looking for anybody in particular?" asked a big orderly. His name tag said *Remundo*. He wore a white shirt, white pants, white sneakers, even a white belt. The mop bucket was his. "Or maybe you're looking for some *thing*?"

Both.

It was uncanny. Now the place was something beyond hospital or prison; now it was *my* past. The room Remundo pointed me to—last door on the left—occupied the same floor-plan location as the boss's office in the basement hall at Gafton College. For an instant I saw, instead of *Grubgeld, N.* on a 3x5 card, a handsomely engraved name plate:

Dr. Norris T. Grubgeld
Chair, Department of Humanities

"My door is always open," he had said on the day he hired me.

But this one in Golden Oaks wasn't; the hinge angle was nowhere close to ninety degrees. I knock-knock-knocked; no one answered; I entered. The bed linen was folded at the foot of the mattress, the television screen dark, the room bare of personal effects. In that moment, I was nearly overcome with the dread that Grubgeld, N. had also chosen today to depart this world, after eating all *his* mashed potatoes.

Back in the hall, I felt weird, disoriented. I needed to find Remundo, but I had the strangest feeling I wasn't going to find him here. Because here was not here. Looking up and down the hall, I was back in that basement at Gafton. Same floor plan. There was cheerful Tatum's office, with a laminated yellow smiley face tacked to his name plate and the guitar case standing upright in a corner by his neat desk. Directly across the hall, Phyllis Lundquist, who kept, beneath the framed diplomas on her wall, her one *Teacher of the Year* plaque, the most overdue and well-deserved award of that kind ever given. And my good friend Isaac Freed, whose door was festooned with clipped comic strips, couplets, adages, epigrams. Weird thoughts ran through my mind. I tell you, for a time, in that nursing home in Billings, Montana, I was back treading the underground at Gafton College. Every day for three school years, I walked that hall—to and from class, bathroom, drinking fountain, micro-wave, supply room (for more *pencils*). Every day for three years I listened to its human sounds:

*I might as well go squat at a stop sign with a piece of card-board—*WILL GRADE FOR FOOD.

The way to get over it is to just picture your audience in their underwear.

Twenty-seven years I've been here; surely that's worth something.

Oh, Libby, you're going to spoil me with these brownies of yours.

And endless giggles from that office right *there*, then a coed's voice, from right *there*, saying, with mock indignation, "No *fair!*"

"That's not fair," I heard someone say just inside a doorway from which one wheel of the yellow mop bucket protruded. This voice protesting the most recent injustice in the world came from the room closest to the D-Wing's locked-from-the-outside double doors. The 3x5 said *Coombs, D.* So I was back in the land of Golden Oaks but soon realized that, in her mind, Coombs, D. was somewhere else. "No fair, Joey," said a woman not all that much older than I am. Except there was no Joey. Just Remundo, mopping the closet-sized bathroom and patiently explaining: "I'm telling you, Miss C., he ain't here; he's long gone." Miss C. or Coombs, D.—or whoever she was at the moment—monitored every move the orderly made. "We can't play this game properly," she insisted, "if you keep hiding in the outhouse. It's no fair."

An odd urgency impelled me. Half breathless, slightly dizzy, I crowded into the doorway with the hide-and-seek player, interrupted her to make my own complaint. "He's not there," I said to Remundo. "The room is empty."

Remundo told Coombs, D. to go look for Joey in the barn, and when she had left us, he smiled a wide-mouthed smile full of big, even teeth. "It's cool, man," he said, mopping in slow motion. "Old Mr. G. ain't gone nowhere we can't find him, not in the five years I been here. Son's a pilot, flies all over the world, but some reason picked Billings for home base. When his old man started losing his marbles, brought him up here from somewhere down South—"

"Nebraska," I said.

"Bingo," Remundo said. "Pilot's an only child, I think. Mother's dead, and he wanted to keep an eye on his pop, I guess."

That's right. He *was* married. The printed invitations to the Christmas parties I didn't attend were from Dr. and *Mrs.* Norris Grubgeld. But I didn't remember a child, had let the crutches become such a symbol of the man that I never considered the possibility. There was a lot I hadn't considered twenty-five years ago.

"Retired something or other at a little college down there," Remundo said, dipping the mop in the bucket's dirty water, hauling it up again, lowering the hanging, dripping strands into the wringer. Every move was slow, slower, slowest, as if he had ahead of him the mopping of every stone atop the Great Wall of China and saw no good reason to rush. "Healthy as a horse, can tell you all about when he was a kid, but he don't remember two minutes ago."

When Coombs, D. came back from trying to find Joey in the barn, Remundo had to send me on my way. "Try the dayroom," he said. "Just follow the hall down past the bend. Can't miss it." So I went beyond the bend and, in the process, past who knows how many barns and cellars and sandlots and gardens and porch swings. And at the end of that hall there was indeed a dayroom—one much too dim for its name. But Remundo was right: Grubgeld, N., husband and father, *hadn't* gone anywhere, except eight hundred miles from Gafton, Nebraska. Even from behind, I recognized the thick black stems of his glasses and the generous ears those stems rested on.

He was in a wheelchair, sitting at a twelve-foot folding table spread with board games and a pile of undisturbed jigsaw pieces. Except for a floor pacer and another wheelchair rider napping in front of a television—this one blessedly muted—Norris Grubgeld was alone. Slowly I moved around the table so as to face him. Like me, with my paunch and receding hairline, my recent colonoscopy and joint stiffness of a morning, he had aged. Nostrils and ears sprouted hair, but the scalp was barren except for a few white strands combed sideways. The skin of his cheeks and neck was looser, the lenses of his glasses thicker. Only his chest and shoulders were unchanged. Even the gray sweater jacket zipped all the way to his throat could not conceal the breadth nor the muscling. During my Gafton days it hadn't occurred to me: He had the upper body of a gymnast. I sat down in a folding chair across from him; he was scooting chess pieces around on a Monopoly board and did not look up.

There were no elbow crutches anywhere close to him. Nor any crutches by either of the other residents. Nor, when I thought about it, had I seen any crutches in the time warp of the hall. Walkers, canes, carts, IV poles—but no elbow crutches. And wheelchairs do not make the sound in question. Yet because of that sound I had been drawn to the D-Wing. And, with Remundo's help, I had found Grubgeld, N. What were the odds? Almost exactly twenty-five years after we had sat across from each other for the last time in my basement office at Gafton College, there I was in a folding chair, sitting across from him again.

"Dr. Grubgeld?" I said as he pushed a king and pawn around Marvin Gardens and Park Place. "Norris?"

Finally he looked up from his game. Through the glinting lenses of his glasses, he studied me across the folding table.

"Norris?" I said, looking hard at those lenses. "Dr. Grubgeld? It's me—Ed Beverly. Do you remember?"

He stared at me until scrutiny gave way to compassion. "But you can't *kill* a king," he explained. "He's only subject to check-mate."

"Do you remember me? Ed Beverly? Edwin?"

Grubgeld peered at me as if mildly perplexed. Then slowly his expression changed, from perplexity to fear, then from fear to anguish. "Papa," he said suddenly, "where's the doctor? My stomach hurts so bad." He took off his glasses and said, "Why did he leave, Papa? Why?"

When he began to cry, I was moved in a way I've never been moved before.

"Papa! Pa-pa!" my old boss said, weeping, "it feels like a knife!" Then he made a fist and slammed the game table so hard half the chess pieces bounced off the Monopoly board and clattered onto the tile floor. "Smash those crutches!" he said, crying, running at the nose, leaking at the mouth, all without the least hint of self-consciousness. "Smash them!"

As abruptly as it had started, the crying stopped. Slowly old Norris Grubgeld brought a sweater sleeve up to his nose, then on to his eyes. In three years' time, I had seen those eyes only through the thickest of lenses. They now grew remarkably clear and penetrating, and he said, in his one and only lucid flash, "I know who you are, Ed Beverly."

Almost thirty years of enmity—over what? Review-Consult-Solidify? The disproportion is staggering! As I sat across from my old boss, the question of my forgiving him or anyone else receded somewhere much farther away than thirty years. In its place came the insistent realization that the only person accountable for my wrongs and my grudges and my vanities was *me*, and that any petition for forgiveness needed to start there.

No, I'm not Prince Judah. But finally—finally—I begin to comprehend his last line. Coming directly from Golgotha in the movie's last scene, Judah enters the once great House of Hur—now dark and run down—and immediately sees Esther waiting for him across the inner courtyard. As he approaches, it is clear that she is standing on the bottom step of a great stairway and is thus positioned slightly above him. His face bespeaks a great unburdening, an unburdening Esther knows for what it is. Wordlessly, he rests his head in the hollow below her bosom, and she cradles him with a maternal tenderness. "Almost the moment he died," Judah says, referring to the young rabbi, "I heard him say, 'Father, forgive them, for they know not what they do. . . .' And I felt his voice take the sword out of my hand." Then the camera moves to take in his mother and sister at the top of that great stairway, and he ascends to meet and embrace them, their reunion made even sweeter with his realization that the lepers are healed and whole, as he now is. The expression on his face in that culminating moment is finally the whole sermon of Christianity.

Dozens of times I've watched that last scene. The moment *always* brings tears. I defy anyone to see it and not be moved. Only afterward, when it fades, does such a feeling get written off as something other than what it has to be if that young rabbi is, as Esther rightly claims, "a man more than a man." For one stark, lingering moment across that game table, I saw Norris Grubgeld's face, and, reflected in his eyes, my face, and both wore exactly the same expression Judah wears there at the end. This was the same expression, incidentally, on the face of the disaffected daughter when I saw her much later that evening. She was sitting in the one easy chair in her little living room in Balford—hadn't gotten up to answer the door—when I suggested maybe it was time to let go of some things she had been holding onto for too long. Perched on an ottoman with a missing caster, staring at the cordless telephone still in her lap, I was more than mindful of what I was asking.

Before that visit, though, I had to take my leave of Norris Grubgeld. Just after I said good-bye, just before I got up from the folding chair to head for home, the muted screen on the day-room television went black. And just like that, the other wheel-chair rider awoke, scrubbed the sleep from his eyes, got his bearings as much as they could be gotten, then slowly wheeled to an open space in the middle of the room. Before I knew it, Norris Grubgeld had put on his glasses, thumbed off his wheel brakes, and was nimbly maneuvering toward the same spot. Checking the floor tiles carefully, the two competitors came to some imaginary starting line. Nine laps around the dayroom? No foul play. No stretcher bearers necessary. They then positioned themselves according to specifications only they could know, gripped a wheel in each hand, and finally—by default, I suppose—looked to me for a signal.

And I obliged.

LIQUIDATING EARL HAWS

N FIELDS ALONG THE BALFORD HIGHWAY, SHAGGY CAT-
tle fed on beet tops frozen black-green in the months since
harvest. Across the snow-swept tracks of digger wheels, urine
puddles and fresh manure steamed like fumaroles. Behind the
wheel of his car, bound alone for the river rim beyond Ralston,
bank vice-president Frett Maxwell Jr. glanced again at the briefcase on the passenger seat. Within a half hour he would rest that
briefcase on a kitchen table, snap open the clasps, and pull out
the blue-label file. Then he would explain to a man who had
farmed almost forty years that "partial" liquidation would spare
the land his father had grubbed out of sagebrush, but not any
machinery to farm it with, and not his herd.

"I've got a heifer ready to calve is the only thing," Earl had said
earlier that morning, "and the weather's turning. But if it's not
something we can cover on the phone right now, you're more
than welcome to come ahead."

One of several things Frett couldn't cover on the phone was
his confession that the selection committee had met a full month
ago, the very end of 1991, and it was his own foot dragging that
had brought him up against the February deadline. Some bankers saw benevolence in rendering a liquidation verdict in the
dead of winter. It had to be easier, they reasoned, to accept the
dwindling profitability of a lifetime of planting and harvesting
when the frost went deep.

"You actually going to do that to a fellow Mormon," Leland
the Lutheran had asked. "On a Friday?" Religion wasn't their

only difference. Frett had just turned fifty-six and would soon celebrate his thirty-second wedding anniversary. Joe Leland was forty and still a bachelor. And, too, he was from Cheyenne—the other corner of the state—and didn't have to know the history of his blue-label files. Even the one thing they had in common, a degree from the University of Wyoming, pointed up more differences: Besides being a die-hard fan of his alma mater's sports teams (lover of game-day parties and a devout collector of memorabilia), Leland lived to bet on winners and losers and point spreads. In fact, wearing a UW visor and a ridiculously oversized UW tie pin, he showed considerably more zeal for organizing the weekly office pool than for his duties as a loan officer in the Farm Credit Division. "Why not have this Earl guy come here?" he had asked as Frett Jr. donned overcoat, galoshes, and the newsboy cap with earflaps. "Gives you the home-court advantage. Because what they don't realize is this is just as hard on us as it is them."

"Executioner's sob story," Pop would have said, right up until his death five years ago. During his three decades as vice-president of Balford Savings and Loan, the man everyone else knew as Big Frett Maxwell had mentored many a subordinate, including the youngest of his nine sons: "If you've got to tell a man you're pulling the plug on him, at least have the guts to do it without hiding behind a desk."

The highway crossed the railroad tracks just beyond the Ralston trestle, curved past a sign listing a population of a hundred people, then widened into the town's main street. Off toward the southwest, toward the river rim and Cody, the sky hung low. Late in college, Frett's idea of a career in banking had not accounted for pulling the plug on anybody. And a lot of practice in recent years hadn't made the job any more palatable. For the last two years, Earl and Ruby had come up short on their payments, a point repeatedly asserted in the late-December selection meeting. Their most impassioned defense had come from Leland, of all people. "But if an old married couple with their payment history isn't a good risk," he said, "who is?"

"It's the times," Pop had said at the beginning of the slide a decade earlier, on the eve of his retirement. With nothing else to blame, you blame the times. But that was more honest than blaming small-farmer "inefficiency," which was the favorite scapegoat in selection meetings these days. Not long before he died, Pop said he hadn't seen such thin profit margins in all the years since 1948, when Grandpa Vanderfisk pledged to make a banker out of an oil man and offered him a big office next to the vault. Thin profit margins favored bigger operators—like Jersey Teague and the DeGraffs and Paul Mendenhall. And, of course, Winn Bingham, who was married to Big Frett's tenth child and only daughter.

Just past the bar and sugar beet factory at the far edge of town, Frett met a very old grain truck chugging toward Balford under its burden of bedsprings, mattresses, a cupboard and bookcase, and a green refrigerator. At least liquidations didn't look like that anymore. Pop used to tell of standing on the main street in Needles, California, one evening in 1938, when a caravan of Okies went through. Pitiful as their goods were, he said, their faces were worse, and he vowed then and there to always position himself and his family on the sure side of life's gambles. So after thus positioning himself during most of the Forties—with the help of a lot of oil money—he accepted Grandpa Vanderfisk's offer and positioned himself as a banker. And for the next thirty years he stayed on one side of the farming gamble by lending money to men on the other.

But to plant a seed at all was to hazard the harvest, and somebody had to do it. At one point early in his life, Frett Jr. had seriously considered positioning himself as one of the willing. He kept that willingness to himself as long as he could. "This Old MacDonald nonsense is not something you want to romanticize,"

Pop said when he found on the report card from Frett's first semester at the university a high mark for a class in Agricultural Methods. That was December 1954, just a month or so before Frett left on his mission. "Let's hope two and a half years trying to convert Japs will knock it out of your system."

And it did—more or less. By the time Frett went back to the university the fall of 1957, the term before he enlisted in the Navy, his interest had shifted all the way from farming . . . to ranching. "I thought you were over all that, Junior," Pop said, unimpressed with that report card's high mark in Range Management. "Let's hope four years crawling with bilge rats cures you for good."

As it turned out, there wasn't much actual bilge duty. After just one deployment from Coronado, he spent the rest of his hitch quartermastering in Texas and Nevada, Pennsylvania and New Jersey, and there at the end, back on the west coast in Washington. But instead of curing his ambition to raise grass-fed beef, those four years stirred it all the more—especially after his marriage halfway through to high school classmate Helen Godwin.

"A farm girl?" Pop said during the telephone conversation announcing the engagement. "Listen, Junior, when you're a long way from home, a letter from *any* female is bound to flip your switch. You're going to want to think this over." The resistance held steady right up to the five-day leave granted for the wedding. "But a farm girl, Junior? Is she the one pushing this harebrained idea of yours to run cattle when you get out of the service?"

No, that harebrained idea belonged to his own flesh and blood.

"Marry who you want to marry, Junior," Pop had finally conceded the night before the ceremony, "but careerwise, I can't stand by and let you dig a dry well." So when honorably discharged E-5 F. Maxwell (petty officer second class) took Helen and their first baby with him back to the university in 1962, he had positioned himself to study financial management. "In thirty years," Pop had said as the last belongings were loaded for the move to Laramie, "you'll thank me."

It wasn't even a year after graduation that Frett was assigned his first farm liquidation file, which was a much rarer kind of file in 1965. "It's a bloody cold chore, no two ways about it," Pop said when he handed over the financial history of a sheepman named Otto Schuyler. "But somebody's got to do it."

So Frett did it. He remembered declining the offer of a cup of tea from Mrs. Schuyler, then opening the file on the little kitchen table, shuffling its contents, fumbling for words. What could be said to a man who had positioned himself so as to dig with bar and shovel every hole for every fence post around an eight-hundred-acre grassy shelf at the base of the McCullough badlands? There were not enough columns of figures on all the bank forms on earth to explain how forty or fifty years of that species of work could bring a man to arrears. Russell Henderson. Jace Tillery. Roy Sebright. They were but recent recipients of the same futile explanation. For collective decades, they had made a quiet and sufficient living on the other side of the gamble. But one by one, as costs rose and prices dropped, they had had to hear from a banker, of all people, that no amount of continued toil could make their livelihoods a paying proposition.

"People have no idea how hard banking actually is," Pop said not long before he died.

To Frett, as he turned at the marker for Road 11, onto gravel overlaid with packed snow, that sentiment didn't sound all that different from the executioner's lament Pop so vehemently scorned.

⟹ ⟸

That wasn't Pop's only inconsistency in reacting to the vagaries of life.

Coming off the highway, Road 11 pointed back east, toward the river. To get to the lane leading south, to Earl Haws's farm, on this cold Friday in January of 1992, Frett had to pass one leading north. At the entrance of that north lane stood an arched stone gateway visible from a mile in any direction. The lettering sculpted into the arch's masonry—BINGHAM FARMS—marked an enterprise that had been anything but a dry well. Who would have thought Patty Dew Maxwell, only daughter of Big Frett the banker, would have ended up married these thirty-four years to Winn Bingham the farmer? In January of 1958, the only thing to be said of a marriage between those two was that it positioned both of them for disaster. At the time, she was eighteen, almost a dozen years younger than the groom. Until just three weeks before the wedding, they had never met. Yet Pop not only accepted the marriage, he arranged and promoted it. One of the only things in their favor that first year was that baby Emery could actually pass for Winn's child. And now baby Emery was thirty-three, a husband and father himself, and a full partner in Bingham Farms.

There were risks worse than farming.

Stories long since forgotten amid the success of Bingham Farms had, in the old days, written Winn off as a vocational failure even before he had a wife with whom he could then prove himself a marital failure as well. In the years right after Arvy Bingham's death in 1953, Winn's reputation came to rest on the neglect of his parents' homestead—which happened to be mortgaged to Balford Savings and Loan—and on his promiscuity and drinking. "Bloody losel," Pop himself had remarked many times, capturing, with language only he would use, an assessment nevertheless shared by all of Balford. So Frett Jr. could never decide whether the town's amnesia about the origin of Bingham Farms confirmed the balm of forgiveness or the appeal of success.

The lead-up to Patty Dew's surprise wedding was, in memory, inseparable from the Hawses' pleasantly *un*surprising wedding.

When Frett came home during the university's fall break of 1957 to attend Earl and Ruby's reception, he didn't travel alone. But his little sister made the trip only after considerable coaxing. Three or four days in Balford meant three or four days apart from her football-player boyfriend in Laramie. In returned-missionary, big-brother Frett's judgment, she was already far too smitten with that third-string halfback from St. Louis, who was not the least bit interested in religion—especially hers, with its stricture regarding chastity. During those weeks of trying, albeit feebly, to reconcile that stricture with what the halfback *was* interested in, Patty Dew couldn't have picked Winn Bingham out of a crowd, much less known that he was pushing thirty with only the decline of his parents' farm to show for it.

Yet by Christmas, not even two weeks after an Albany County Justice of the Peace sat at his desk in the Laramie courthouse and said he could not be expected to conduct a wedding without a groom, Pop had decided Wild Winn was just the man for his only daughter. He might as well have announced the abolition of interest on all bank loans forevermore. After the halfback, Pop would have met any other losel's interest in his only daughter with a cocked shotgun. And of course he had to relax his opposition to banker-farmer romantic pairings, at least long enough to orchestrate this one.

Pop could hardly take credit for the success of Winn and Patty's marriage, but that success wasn't hindered at all by the success of the farm—most of which, at least early on, he could take credit for. Domestic comforts, vehicles, buildings, machinery, and the first of much new property to augment Arvy Bingham's homestead acreage—Pop kept his end of the bargain: If Wild Winn would marry Patty in her hour of reproach, if he would shed that nickname and the habits behind it, Big Frett Maxwell would see to the funding.

All's fair in love and banking.

At the big, fatted-calf wedding feast at the Maxwell residence, Pop made a characteristic show of presenting the couple with a reservation for two weeks at a Florida beach resort. Not so characteristic, however, was his interaction with Winn's mother, who was frankly troubled by the marriage. Late in the afternoon, just before the wedding party moved outdoors and down to the frozen pond for bonfires and wagon rides, Pop found Etha Bingham at a small corner table picking at a slice of wedding cake. He asked if he, Big Frett the banker, could join her, widow of small farmer Arvy Bingham. Only when she said yes did he pull up a chair. Then he looked her in the eye, and said, "God has given us both a fair-to-middling shot of seeing beauty from ashes in this thing, and I pledge my heart and means to that end."

It seemed as if there ought to be something in the whole matter to hold against Pop. Yet Frett had never quite found it in his motive and, granting the motive, not even in his method.

⇒　⇐

At the entrance to Earl's lane there was no stone arch—only a battered mailbox nailed to an off-plumb corner post and, fifty feet beyond that post, the hump of a culvert. Crossing that hump today seemed to pull memory up by the roots. It was that same fall, 1957 (the season when Pop wished for his youngest son an enlightening association with bilge rats), that the Haws place had passed from father to son, forty years after Foley Haws had plowed its first acres out of sagebrush. Within a few years at either end, this was the timeline of the Bingham place.

Back in the fifties, the only difference between the two farms lay in the promise of their heirs. Brains, ambition, industry—Earl was the one with the makings of the success story. Yet, thirty-five years later, he was the one being liquidated.

Which is exactly what would have happened to Winn Bingham all those years earlier—if not for Earl Haws. Without Earl's neighborliness, there wouldn't have been even a marginal farm for Pop to sponsor, let alone a marginal farmer to recruit as a son-in-law. In the old days, this or that seasonal need on the Bingham farm was common news and commonly elicited the help of brethren from church. This help was given with surprisingly durable generosity and good cheer, with only the rarest murmur regarding Arvy's spotty self-reliance. Mostly folks made allowance because of his heart problems and because he and his wife did what they could do. But when Arvy died, the winter of 1953, so did the quorum service projects on the Bingham place. Because the son's shortfalls resulted from traits and habits very different from the father's, they had a very different effect on the goodwill of others.

In the years right after Arvy's death, even the day-to-day work of the farm became a succession of emergencies. The crops and cattle were always overdue for some sort of attention. Increasingly, the tenor of the whole enterprise became desperation. Etha, who by then was well into her sixties, did what she could to plug holes in the dike, but she had only so many fingers. Time and again, Earl came to the rescue. Time and again, the dike held.

The last emergency, before the farm took an astonishing turn for the better, came during the bean harvest of 1957, which happened also to be the season of Earl and Ruby's wedding. No sooner had Earl brought his bride home from a one-day, late-September honeymoon in Jackson Hole than he pulled a brand new combine out of his own rain-delayed harvest and, with wind and frost in the offing, went to save Winn's. Despite her gratitude, Etha was plagued with the realization that next fall, barring a drastic change in her son, there might be nothing left to save. That's why, on the second day of January, 1958, she went to Earl and offered him lease-to-own rights on her property. Unbeknownst to her, however, the drastic change had begun—with incentives from none other than Big Frett Maxwell. The biggest of those incentives explained why, on the morning after his mother's offer, Winn hurried down Earl's lane and retracted it.

⇒ ⇐

What if Earl had had a sponsor like Pop?

"If farming's the same crapshoot for everybody," the hovering Leland had remarked this morning, with his bucket-sized UW coffee mug in hand, "why is it the bush leaguers we always end up liquidating?"

The lane narrowed to a pair of tracks between two walls of plowed snow, high as the car's roof. At the point where the lane cleared the plowed channel and turned onto the lip of the rim itself, the land fell abruptly away, down and down, under the pewter sky, to a river blanketed at its bends by a cold fog. It had been many years since Frett had seen those swampy pasture terraces shellacked with ice. High over the great rises and runs of the slope, a hawk rode the winter wind.

Snow had begun to fall. Through a strange peephole in the sky's gray ceiling, the weak January sun painted the river in gauzy, silvery flashes. When the younger half of the Maxwell boys saw sleds under the tree, the Christmas of 1947, they immediately thought of the pasture ice and of the steward most convenient to them, farm boy Earl Haws. Earl was sixteen at the time—a year older than the twins and three years older than Boyd. Frett himself hadn't yet turned twelve.

"But he says it's okay," said Merrill.

"Honest, Pop," said Ferrill.

"It's not Earl making the payments," Pop had said. "Foley's the one you got to ask."

On such a lane on such a morning, caution was already the imperative. But now Frett slowed the car to a crawl and gave his gaze almost entirely to the topography between the rim fence and the river. He felt again the snagging of pants during the straddle-crossing of the middle strand of barbed-wire, the knee jolts from the long downslope hike, dodging sagebrush and Russian olives, tacking and slewing, all the way to the bottom terrace. He smelled again weenies and bologna roasted over deadwood fires, tasted soup and hot chocolate from mess-kit cups.

He remembered the host's dress and gear. Instead of mittens, Earl wore double-layered wool socks with a thumb hole, compensated broken overshoe buckles with twine and tape, guided his sheet of rusty tin with a wire leash, like a bucket bail, twist-tied at each end to a chisel-punched corner hole. While such improvisation did not charm Frett's older brothers as it did him, even they were grudgingly impressed. Despite their proper winter clothing, despite the varnished yokes and new-rope leashes and waxed runners of brand new gift sleds, even the twins—able athletes, both of them—could never outrace Earl Haws.

The bottom terrace was the only one suitable for sledding. Its sheet of ice was unmarred by rock veins or candied streaks or even the occasional stump or hummock. More important, it extended to the very brink of the river. Flirting with that brink, in the final arcing sweep of a thousand sled runs, stood in Frett's memory as the ideal boyhood challenge. Despite the embellishments of bravado, the drop from brink to river was quite modest, and, though swift enough to resist freezing in all but the coldest temperatures, the winter current ran only knee-deep. It was mortal thrill without mortal risk.

But he didn't actually go over the edge until ten years later, during that young adult sledding party in February of 1958—just a few months after Earl's wedding, a few weeks after Patty Dew's, a few days before boot camp and the hoped-for proximity to bilge rats. And, Frett remembered, it was on the occasion of his third date with Helen.

"Isn't that Warner Godwin's daughter?" Pop had asked after finally prying her name out of his youngest son. The report card with the commendable mark in Range Management still rested on the desk in Pop's study, as if quarantined. "Doesn't he farm?"

"Yep," Frett remembered saying, "that's what the man does. Just a couple of miles up the highway from where your new son-in-law farms."

They had looked at each other a long time. "Okay," Pop said. "Okay. No need to get lippy about it." But that was the extent of either censure or defensiveness. The tableau of that moment was still clear. For one rare instant, Pop's certainty faltered and, with it, his sway and authoritativeness. He became reflective, maybe even meek. Then, in an unprecedented and unduplicated and, as it turned out, unremembered concession, Pop said, almost whispering, "I don't suppose there's any way to make a start in anything in this world without *some* kind of risk. And the only human antidote I know for that is love."

Unconsciously, Frett had stopped the car. His rubber-booted right foot rested heavily on the brake pedal.

On that day in February thirty-four years earlier, three couples had positioned themselves for a run down the smooth ice of that bottom pasture terrace—two of them on proper sleds, and the third, on a rusty sheet of tin. To Ruby and Patty Dew and Helen, this was a maiden flight. A rope leash for two of the steersmen and wire for the third, and someone near the deadwood fire yelled, "May the best man lose!"

Once started, the downward motion could not be stopped. Once committed, the riders could not turn back. Not to the beginning, not to the point of the first crouching and settling, the first awkward scooting, the giving over of the sled's burden to gravity. From that point, there was only holding on and being held, in tandem, and navigating the long slope together. Two pregnant wives and a girl who wound up being courted mostly through letters from Navy bases. "I'll support you in whatever you decide to do," Helen wrote, giving voice to one of the oldest and fondest of all commonplaces. "Whatever comes our way, we'll face it together." Down and down the couples raced into bright sunlight glinting off ice, the cold air numbing chins and cheeks, young men sawing at the steering leashes, young women shrieking with laughter. Farmers and bankers. Ice was no respecter of persons.

"Why would I do that to myself?" Leland always said in answer to the most ubiquitous question of all in a town like Balford. "Getting hitched is taking a huge chance."

Caution, prudence, foresight. Yes. On a bright winter morning thirty-four years ago, Patty Dew and Ruby were both pregnant, both due in six months, both wholly amenable to the fifty-fifty possibility of the sons who would be born within a week of each other. At that early point in motherhood, they didn't need to be flying off edges and into rivers, as their husbands well knew when they dropped their heavy heels and sent up a spray of ice crystals. When their motion had slowed sufficiently, each pair bailed off, quite gracefully, and slid to a stop long before the brink. Thirty-four years later, against the long odds of life, they were still married.

It wasn't the prospect of an easy sledding victory that had delayed Frett's final, braking arc until it was too late. Even without competition, the only thing that emboldened him to fly beyond the brink, to pit security against insecurity, was Helen and her way of holding on and steadying at the same time.

Holding on for dear life.

⇒ ⇐

At the small orchard marking the entrance into Earl's yard, Frett slowed for a bend, drove past the garden plot, past the fuel tanks beneath a big cottonwood, then stopped between a cedar-log shop and a machinery shed. Arvy had built both half a century earlier. The newer shop and grain bin were added during Earl's tenure. And that's where the improvements would end. Unlike

Emery Bingham, the oldest Haws boy had showed no interest in farming, nor had any of his siblings.

Frett turned off the engine. With the heater fan stopped, there was nothing to keep the cold at bay. With the wipers stilled, the windshield soon grew obscure. He snugged the cap on his head, the gloves on his hands, then slipped his fingers through the handle of the briefcase and climbed stiffly out of the car. The wind lashed his face, even stronger and colder than he had expected. But on that wind he caught a whiff of fireplace smoke before he saw any drifting from the chimney. Turning up the collar of his overcoat, he followed a crusted path to a door just off the kitchen. He knocked. Through a window he saw, on a kitchen counter, a crock-pot plugged in and, beside it, a bowl of rising bread dough. He knocked again.

Stepping away from the door, he looked through the living room window. He remembered that fireplace from the day of the sledding party. He could still picture where Helen, wrapped in a quilt, had stood in front of the roaring blaze. Similarly wrapped, he had been in no hurry for their outer clothing to dry. He remembered her flushed cheeks, her combed wet hair, remembered her shifting the quilt around her shoulders so as to free a hand to accept a cup of hot chocolate from Earl's mother. That shifting afforded a wonderfully substantial glimpse of her long-john bottoms.

Maybe Earl and Ruby had surmised the purpose of a visit they didn't want to sit through after all. He turned, retraced his steps to the car, and opened the door. He could call Earl later and apologize for missing him, and reschedule. Or he could invite him to make the trip to the bank after all—and thus regain the home-court advantage. Either way, he faced the disagreeable task of reporting his failure to a subordinate; whatever the matter at hand, Leland knew neither tact nor deference. "But what really baffles me about the Mormon religion, way more than the gambling rule," he had said as recently as yesterday, when Frett declined for the thousandth time to venture a wager in the weekly office pool, "is this thing against coffee and tea."

The snow was coming down harder. Lunch was slow-cooking. Chimney smoke indicated a well-laid fire. Car and truck were both parked in their places. And neither Earl nor Ruby would hide in a house while a visitor called at their kitchen door. They would not do that. That's when he saw, past the grain bin, a line of tracks already filling and fading. He tossed the briefcase on the driver's seat and turned away from the door even as he pushed it closed. If you've got to tell a man you're pulling the plug on him, don't hide behind a desk or telephone. Or a steering wheel.

The fast-disappearing tracks led toward a barn thirty yards away, a low structure with a flat roof. Parked along its north wall were a steel-wheeled dump-rake, a one-row potato planter, and a mowing machine, all obsolete for several decades, all half-buried from the last storm. More precisely, the tracks led to the far corner of this north wall. No evidence of milling about, or skirting, or retracing. The footprints just stopped. Frett looked up to rule out rope or ladder or whirlwind into heaven. Only then did he notice the rusted hinge straps and the stub of a thin latch lever protruding between two planks.

The click and creak of the door's hardware were swallowed by the wind. For a moment, after stepping over the threshold and closing the door, Frett simply stood, grateful for a wall between him and the weather. But this wall had no windows. And though the middle third of the barn's south side was a broad opening into the corral beyond, that opening stood forty feet distant. On either side of that opening was a short section of front wall. Such light as was admitted between those sections and the low roof barely reached this deep into the shelter.

In the dimness, Frett Jr. got his bearings. He stood in a narrow alley running between the barn's side wall and a hay bunk.

On the other side of the bunk, a dozen cattle stood in fresh straw and stared warily at his intrusion. Gradually, the smell of manure and cud chewing and animal warmth enveloped him. The last time he had been in—or on—this barn must have been a quarter century ago. "These aren't banker hours, Brother Frett," someone had said when he showed up early on a Saturday for an elders quorum roofing party, a service project Earl never requested or even agreed to. But he didn't run them off, either. First, the old straw thatch had to come off, then the sagging woven wire which for so long had supported it. Then they nailed thick runners across the roof timbers, then thinner runners across those. And finally they laid the tin. Besides several other farmers, the crew included a plumber and shoe clerk, an electrician and math teacher, and a welder and insurance salesman. But a banker in a nail apron and fishing hat was probably the biggest incongruity of all. And to think he was once embarrassed at a ward apple-picking by Pop's too-blue bib overalls and penny loafers.

Even inside the barn, it was very cold. With eyes adjusted to the dimness, Frett could see his breath, but no tracks—only the forty-foot alley leading to a few stacked hay bales and an apparent dead-end. Still, he moved in that direction—past the last three plastic-wrapped salt licks on a pallet, past a saddle on a sawhorse, past a very old motorcycle with no seat. The cold dust stirred by his galoshes powdered the hems of his slacks and overcoat. Hanging from a spike on the wall, between a singletree and a scythe, was a Balford Savings and Loan calendar from July 1982. In six months—ten years from that calendar date—this barn would be empty.

"But seriously," Leland had asked between sips from his gigantic UW mug, "why do this?"

The wind moaned. A sheet of tin flapped at the seam. Even nails well driven could work loose over a lifetime. With their big, unblinking eyes, the cows followed Frett's movement. And his movement followed the feed bunk, to where it ended at the section of wall to the right of the barn's opening.

Again, Frett Jr. stood baffled. He was cold, and, as the cattle would agree, alien in this place. More than one bad dream in his life had had him in a room with no door, a tent with no flap, a basement with no stairway. But those were dreams. One night last month, headed to the bathroom in the stupor of interrupted sleep, he had become disoriented in the darkened hallway and wound up groping for a familar jamb and light switch at the wrong end of the hall. "It's called old age," Helen had teased the next morning.

Just to the right of the feed bunk, he saw it—a panel sticking out slightly from the rest of the wall. It was a door. But it had to be known to be seen. As to width and pattern of placement, its planks matched those of the wall almost exactly—and, at the same time, overlaid and hid the 2x6 frame boards top and bottom, left and right. No hinges, no latch. The top 2x6 was beveled so as to ride—and slide—on the receiving bevel of a board bolted to the wall. Midway up the door's right edge was a well-worn vertical slot whose purpose was no longer a mystery. Into that slot Frett Jr. fit the fingers of his gloved right hand and pulled. Against the soughing of the wind, the sound of bevel sliding on bevel did not register.

No sooner had he made a sufficient opening than he heard a sound that did register:

"Something about a Charolaise's genes makes big shoulders and hips."

"Why put him in with the heifers, then?"

"He's a good bull. Maybe a little hormonal—but you don't spend that kind of money on one just to have him *befriend* them."

"Spoken just like a man."

The laughter rang out warm against the sounds of the day.

Frett stepped through the opening and found himself now behind the trough and stanchion of a snug little pen built as a lean-to against the bigger barn. The pen was dimly lit by a single fly-specked bulb. Beneath that bulb, Earl sat in the muck at the tail end of a prostrate but wild-eyed brindle heifer. His coveralls bore big patchy stains, and the fringe of his stocking cap was beaded with sweat. In each hand he gripped the end of a baling twine. The other ends noosed the protruding front hooves just above the tiny dewclaws. In a scarf and a man's denim coat, Ruby Haws knelt beside him. They did not notice their visitor.

Then the heifer's tail lifted, and her loin contracted.

"Here we go again," Earl said, taking a loop around each hand and drawing evenly on the twines. "Maybe this time will do it."

Steadily, he leaned and pulled, pulled and leaned. When that effort did nothing but scoot the heifer's hind quarters through soiled straw, Ruby sat down directly behind him, in tandem. She reached for the twines, had to settle for the cuffs of his coveralls, and pulled with him, pulled until both began to list, pulled for dear life.

To plant anything was to hazard the harvest, and no one was exempt.

When the calf's shoulders finally slipped the bottleneck of the pelvis, and the unexpectedly smaller hips followed instantly thereafter, the force of united pulling was suddenly released. Amid a gush of birth fluid, Earl and his wife sprawled in the muck, with the new calf, slick as an otter, staring at them.

"Oh my!" Ruby exclaimed delightedly. "Look at that!"

For one last sweet moment, Frett Maxwell Jr. delayed announcing himself. While Earl peeled the caul away from the forehead and cleared mucus from the perfect little nostrils, Ruby stroked the steaming wet flank. Suddenly she leaned and kissed her husband's cheek. Moaning proprietarily, all travail forgotten, mother heifer found her feet and turned to her nudging and licking. Under the rough caresses of her tongue, the calf flapped its ears and made a start.

THE LAST BLESSING OF
J. GUYMAN LEGRAND

S AY THE NAME J. GUYMAN IN THIS PART OF WYOMING,
and any Mormon older than I am will start quoting bits of
a patriarchal blessing given at his hand. This is not horoscope
or palm reading; this is a *blessing*. So just out of reverence, such
quoting ought to be a more private affair than it sometimes is.
But you can't really blame people, not when so many promises
through the years have turned out, especially the unlikely ones.
The spinster marries. The barren wife conceives. The prodigal
comes home. All in the Lord's due time—which can be a long
time, for sure—but all foretold nonetheless.

By the time I had my turn in the ladder-back chair in his tidy
parlor—June 1978—Stake Patriarch J. Guyman LeGrand had been
giving blessings for forty-four years. Figuring from the day in 1934
when he was ordained by a visiting apostle, that period covers
two full generations of Mormons, including my parents and my
older sisters—Afton Rae, Leona, and Eden. The way it works in
the Church, he was not paid a dime for this service; he earned his
living as a machine foreman at the sugar-beet factory in Ralston.

At some point in those forty-four years, the recording method
changed from his wife's stenography to a tape recorder, and
Brother J. Guyman retired from the sugar-beet factory. And
somewhere along the way, he wore out three or four Sunday
suits and turned into an old man. But the blessings kept coming
as powerful as ever. Hundreds of them—given in the same little
house in Balford, by the same priesthood authority, to an endless

line of young people with the same hope for the future lighting their eyes. Thousands of them—all transcribed by Sister LeGrand on the same old typewriter, mailed out in the same timely fashion.

Only one thing made mine any different.

It was the last one he gave.

At sixteen, I couldn't know that he would lay his fairly steady, ninety-seven-year-old hands on my head one Sunday afternoon, address me in full—Everett Tolbert Godwin—pronounce my patriarchal blessing, and be dead by that evening. At sixteen, I couldn't know that within thirty years after feeling those hands on my head, dry as papyrus, I'd lose my dad, then the farm, and now my mother, and wind up, at age forty-six, working as an inspector for County Weed and Pest. None of which, by the way, was anything my blessing gave me to expect.

What I did know, sitting in my Sunday clothes in that ladder-back chair, was that the things Brother J. Guyman LeGrand said by the power of his priesthood office surged through my scalp and down my spine. With my arms folded and eyes closed, it was as if there weren't any years between the Ever Godwin in that chair and the one who would provide for a wife and children through tillage and reaping, gleaning the comforts and necessities of life on land entrusted to him by his fathers. Those were the words. It was a strange and sobering thing to be sixteen and feel no distance of time between me and my progeny.

Or between me and my progenitors, either. By the summer of 1978, my grandpa Warner Godwin had been dead eleven years; I hardly remembered him. But during the giving of the blessing, I could *see* him wresting that land from the wilderness. That was the verb that came out of Brother J. Guyman's mouth. I saw this wresting as Grandpa Godwin grubbing and burning sagebrush below the canal Loop—which he'd helped dig with a team and slip scraper—and my dad, in his boyhood, endlessly picking and piling and hauling off rock. To credit myself with some part in the wresting, I imagined jabbing my irrigating shovel upright between the grubbing hoe and rock sledge.

Tillage and reaping, wresting and entrusting. That's what the blessing says. Not failed farmer hired as a weed inspector because he happened to have a college degree in Ag Econ. At eighteen, I didn't want to go to school at all, BYU or anywhere else. I planned to farm and didn't much like pulling out on Labor Day, leaving my dad with eighty acres of unharvested beans. But my going meant everything to my mother.

Ag Econ! That's rich. Just because several cousins on her side of the family were getting master's degrees in business administration didn't mean that's what I had to do. So—Ag Econ. If you're really going to farm—and not just loan money to farmers or sell them insurance or machinery or, in my case, police their weeds—you can pretty much boil eight semesters of lectures and textbooks down to this: *Spend less than you make.* My dad saw that law as being etched so deep in stone even a patriarchal blessing couldn't counter it. But when things started going bad for us, I really half expected a divine overriding. I cited precedents. What about the spinster or the prodigal? My dad said, "Don't you think, from God's angle, they might have a little better claim on a miracle?"

My dad asked that question at breakfast on the day the blood clot in his leg broke loose and drifted toward his heart. He was loading the hopper of the barley drill, down in a field we called the milkweed patch—to honor the one crop it could make with any predictable abundance. The doctor likened the effect to a gob of mud hitting the fins in a water pump. Boom. The aortic valve sort of exploded. My dad was sixty-nine.

I held on for three more years, but there was no divine overriding. The only definite change in my prospects came when the man from FHA's Denver office showed up one morning to tell me it was time to call it quits.

"It's a blessing in disguise," my mother said. "You can finally use that college degree I talked you into getting and make a steady *salary*."

I've never told her, but there isn't much about Ag Econ you need to know to drive around in a county pickup espying weeds. My patriarchal blessing does not mention turning into an offender for a word, which is pretty much how farmers regard the weed inspector. I know. They suffer him wandering their side roads and scrutinizing their plant life for one reason: so he'll sign the "Weed Release" they need in order to sell their crops. *You might want to nip that little patch on the ditch bank before it seeds out, Dean. Say, Harold, have you tried Roundup in that paddock of yours?* Of course, the farmer is the one who has to do the actual nipping or spraying before the release is granted. In the five years since I lost the farm, I haven't touched a machete or spray nozzle. I advise. I consult. I sign with a flourish. Everett T. Godwin. Serving agriculture in the Shoshone Valley. Smiling picture, with the whole Weed and Pest gang, in the New Year's edition of the *Balford Clarion*.

"Could be, with the Pearly Gates calling, old J. Guyman wasn't at the top of his game," my uncle Eb told me one time. Uncle Eb's a Jack Mormon and prides himself on a nose for doctrinal soft spots. If you don't believe in the idea of God knowing you and everything that's coming, then saying a farm kid will take over his dad's place is nothing more than prediction. But I *do* believe. On the very day I graduated with my degree in Ag Econ, I told my parents I had decided: I wanted to come home and farm. I was twenty-four, unmarried, and not the least bit tempted by a steady salary.

My dad was delighted. As we took our pictures outside the graduation hall, he said, "With your brain and my backbone, we ought to be able to earn the porridge." Between his hat line and his poorly knotted necktie was a face ruddy with windburn, shaved maybe twice a week, not counting Sundays and graduations. After the wet combing wore off, his thinning hair was always at odds with his scalp. Yet, as he stood among students and professors in their robes and hoods, there wasn't an envious or apologetic bone in his body.

My mother was not so delighted. She waited as long as she could, between the picture taking and lunch, before she said, "I hope you've given this a lot of thought, Ever. You could still apply for a master's."

I had given it a lot of thought, and I gave it some more that night. While my parents slept in the back seat, I drove their car on the long road home to our corner of Wyoming, toward the farm and what I thought my life was going to be. Just before he laid hands on my head, Brother J. Guyman, patriarch and retired machine foreman, felt it meet—as he put it—to clarify two points. First, he said, "Don't blame God for war and cleft palates." Then, regarding the line of inspiration from God to the patriarch to the person in the ladder-back chair, he gave me this counsel: "Any troubleshooting regarding what is said and what is understood had best commence at the bottom of the chain."

☞   ☜

For my mother, the surest sign of my blessing's divinity would have been for my future in farming never to have been mentioned in the first place. Every chance she got, from the time I went to Brother J. Guyman until I left home three years later for my mission in the Philippines, she made that feeling known.

"Ever, you don't want to farm," she said on raw March evenings when my dad and I came in from riding cabless tractors. "Go get a college degree, for heaven's sake. Train your mind for office work." As my dad and I peeled off coats and coveralls, and jockeyed for the hot spot in front of the gas stove, she said, "Are you even listening to me?"

Yes, but I was in no mood to question my destined livelihood. Nights like that held too many rewards—the pleasant ache in the palm from the steering wheel knob, the warmth creeping back into my limbs, pork chops and boiled potatoes and bubbling-hot gravy waiting on the table, the good smell of baking-powder biscuits just out of the oven. Office work! The thought was repugnant.

My dad's brothers all ended up away from the farm, and I wouldn't have traded places with any of them, certainly not Uncle Eb and his ditch riding or Uncle Gurn roustabouting in the oil field. To me, even Uncle Rector cruising Balford's streets in his snazzy police car was no step up. When he told his story of lying to the Navy recruiter about his age, he meant to emphasize the lucky timing of Pearl Harbor, how enlistment spared him another summer of weeding and irrigating for Grandpa. I never understood why farming fared so badly in his comparisons.

Or in my mother's. After family reunions at Aunt Helen's big house, my mother was despondent for a week. For therapy, she rearranged furniture, beat rugs, and scrubbed everything in sight. "Your sister certainly did well for herself," she often remarked to my dad, referring to Aunt Helen's marriage to Uncle Frett Jr., the banker.

On those cold spring nights, when I wouldn't question farming, my mother turned to my dad. "Tell him, Tolbert. Tell him he doesn't want to be out in the wind the rest of his life."

"I don't know, Mina. There's worse places."

"And my patriarchal blessing says—"

"I *know* what it says, Ever."

And she did. She and my dad had sat with me that Sunday afternoon in Brother J. Guyman's parlor, his last afternoon on earth. When the official copy of my blessing came in the mail, my mother right away retyped it herself, on carbon paper; she needed enough copies to complete the family sets she gave us all for Christmas that year. I wonder sometimes if her fingers paused, itching to make changes, when she came to that paragraph about tillage and reaping.

"Uggh! This heat," she said on hot July nights, sitting close to the screen door and fanning herself with a *Reader's Digest*. "Tell him, Tol. Tell him he needs to get out of the sun. Tell him what it'll do to him."

"I don't know, Mina."

"And my blessing says—"

My mother had her reasons for feeling the way she felt. *Her* patriarchal blessing said she would refine her musical talents and use them as an ambassador for the gospel. In her middle teens she came to believe that particular line meant she might someday sing in the Tabernacle Choir. At the very least, it seemed to mean she would put a lot of distance between herself and her dad's pig farm over by Cowley, and that was promise enough for her. She had a good voice; in just three quarters of college she took all the singing classes BYU offered. One of her teachers said she had the makings of a professional and arranged to send her to Chicago to prove it.

But a couple of months before she was to go, she met my dad at a stake dance in Lovell. He was just home from the Army. Before long, in accordance with another part of her blessing, she was convinced he was the worthy spouse she was supposed to share the fortunes of life with. And so she did. I have in mind forever a picture of my parents sitting at the kitchen table with pencil and paper, green FHA Farm Budget Planner, and a stack of bills.

"I don't *know* where it's going to come from, Mina."

"Well, I don't either, Tolbert."

The greater the uncertainty, the more she sewed and patched, grew and canned, plucked and stewed. One year, to follow a magazine's prescribed schedule for planting raspberries, she had me in the garden plot in the middle of a spring snowstorm with a spade and bucket of water. In the constricted oval of her scarfed face, her nose dripped like a pipe leak. "Some August," she said against the wind, "when you're enjoying your breakfast berries with cream and sugar, you're going to thank me."

My mother's sharing of fortune cost her more than just hard frugality; she never quite made peace with her lot. At church everybody appreciated her good voice, so she was called on pretty regularly to sing in sacrament meeting, at wedding receptions and harvest-dinner talent shows. But that sort of singing is not the Tabernacle Choir. And she never got to Chicago. Once in a while she spoke of how lucky we were to have what truly matters, the blessings money can't buy, the sort of things people say in testimony meeting. But most of the time she masked her feelings for the farm behind a defensiveness. Didn't coaches and scoutmasters know that some people actually had to *work* in the summer? Did activity planners think the whole world got off at five o'clock? Catch her in a certain mood, and the ticket to heaven was calluses and a backbone crippled sore from field work.

From time to time, frugality became deprivation. Why didn't *we* ski or snowmobile in the winter? Or head for warmer places, to golf or ride sand dunes or whatever she pictured people doing in the name of fun? Why didn't *we* have hobbies? She always asked that question after one of Uncle Rector's visits. He liked to hunt pheasants on my dad's place—he and Uncle Frett—and made a habit of stopping by every few weeks in the summer to see what was growing in the fields and how much bird cover to expect come fall. He always had a new story about hauling Aunt Lib's silly dog to some show in Billings or bowling in the town league or riding the square dancing circuit. During the leanest stretches every year, despite the language of her blessing, my mother made out like my dad was the one standing between her and *better* fortunes.

"Other farmers find a way to take off, Tol. The Binghams and Teagues are always going up to their cabins to boat and fish—where it's cool. Why don't we ever do that?"

"The Binghams and Teagues have things I don't have, Mina."

"Like what?"

"Like a boat and cabin, for starters."

It didn't matter that she wouldn't have known what to do with leisure if she'd had any. My mother in a nylon snow suit? In a golf skirt and visor? I can't feature that. This is a woman who had slopped and docked and clipped needle teeth by the time she was ten years old. Don't misunderstand me. She had faith in patriarchal blessings, her own and her children's. She did. But she could be pretty selective in how she read them. She naturally loved any mention of missionary service or temple marriage or keeping the faith. But the older she got, the more she loved phrases she could read as guarantees of success and fulfillment. Whatever her definition of those two things, she went to her grave thinking they had eluded her.

⟋ ⟋

She didn't want them to elude her children. And if they didn't elude any of her children, if all four of us turned out successful and fulfilled, then maybe she could make a vicarious claim.

That's why she told Afton Rae not to let *anything* distract her from heeding the phrase in *her* patriarchal blessing about applying herself to her studies—and, in the process, earning a full scholarship to BYU. And nothing did, not even the returned-missionary son of Jersey Teague, one of the biggest farmers in the valley. The kid really liked her and was every bit the stalwart son of Zion promised in Afton's blessing. But a couple of weeks into the relationship he made the mistake of confiding that he planned to take his place on his dad's dairy.

"Afton, you don't want to get up at four o'clock the rest of your life to milk a herd of cows."

So with tears fresh from the breakup, my sister went off to BYU, where, in her second year, she met Bennett. After the fourth date, she called home.

"An optometrist!" my mother said into the telephone. The stirring or beating or chopping for the supper pot stopped cold, and I heard her say, "Oh, my." Career choice was all she needed to know about this guy named Bennett. Returned missionary, active in the Church, a young man of honorable intentions? Yes, yes, yes. But *optometrist*! That clinched it. What better guarantee of comforts and necessities? Of getting out of the weather and off the farm? And that's what Bennett was doing. He grew up himself on a wheat farm in Agate, Colorado. Just as long as he didn't plan to take Afton back to it, that upbringing was a bonus to my mother. It meant his folks wouldn't look down on the daughter-in-law's upbringing; it meant Bennett knew calluses.

Kayle C. Lowder was a little different story.

"A lawyer!" my mother said when Leona telephoned.

Kayle Lowder was from Costa Mesa, California—which meant he suffered a sore backbone, when he suffered any bodily discomfort at all, from too much surfing. But, eight hundred miles from the beach, he didn't have to worry about surfing during summer school at BYU. From the moment he and my sister met at a pool party at their bishop's house out in Orem—after a couple of Kayle's impressive backflips off the diving board—they knew they were more than just compatible. So she brought him home in early August 1979, only a little over a year after J. Guyman's death.

"So, Kayle, do you have hobbies?" my mother asked at supper on the first day of their visit.

He said his patriarchal blessing promised the means and opportunity to enjoy life to the fullest. "So, yes, Sister Godwin," he said, "you could say I take my hobbies pretty seriously."

She was already smiling at the way this tanned wonder from the land of beach food was shoveling in *her* roast and rolls and fresh green beans, but now she beamed and said, "Just call me Mina."

To that point in the visit, Just-Call-Me-Mina had spent her time apologizing—for our pair of smoldering burn barrels, for the chopping block and outhouse (with assurances that we did have a bathroom *inside*), for the kitchen's slightly intestinal smell from several days of canning green beans. But now, as she looked from Kayle the Complimenter to Leona the Lucky, she could beam and relax. If hobbies were in his blessing, he was destined to be a good provider. And coming so far just to meet her country folks must mean he had all but decided Leona was the one he wanted to provide for.

After supper, in his California shorts and an old pair of my dad's irrigating boots, Kayle stood swatting deerflies on the ditch bank while I moved water on a cornfield. He caught me looking at him.

"City slicker, huh?"

As long as he knew his place in my cornfield, he was okay. I couldn't find anything not to like about him. When we were introduced, he had even complimented my name. "*Ever*? Like never-ever? That's gnarly."

But then, out in the field, after watching me for a while, he asked, "So do you really *like* farming, Ever?"

Ah-hah! Let him stand five minutes on a ditch bank instead of a surfboard, suffer a few fly bites, and the California beach kid was bound to come out after all.

"What's not to like?"

"Nothing," he said, without stooping to my tone. "There's nothing not to like, Ever. You've got a good life here. You really do." He hesitated. "But will it be enough thirty years down the road? That's all I'm saying."

What does that mean—*enough*? I'm still wondering. According to Kayle and his patriarchal blessing, it meant hobbies, of course. But, as he confided there on the ditch bank, it also meant his mission to a foreign people (in Italy), the rest of his education (in law school), and a life of rewarding toil with Lowder, Lowder, and Son, the law firm his grandpa had started during the Depression. Kayle's future was set. Someday soon he would file lawsuits for people cheated by big companies and share the good things of the earth with a lovely daughter of God.

"And now, because of her, I'm standing in a cornfield in Wyoming!" said Kayle Lowder, laughing and happy. "Isn't it amazing how the Lord keeps his promises?"

⇒   ⇐

The success and fulfillment of her two oldest daughters gave my mother high hopes for her third—until Eden made her call home.

"He sells *what*?" my mother asked.

What kind of guy believes goat-whey lotion is his ticket to wealth? And how does that one guy, out of thousands, wind up married to my sister?

Eden was different from Afton and Leona. She liked the farm. When we were little, and young enough not to understand how things work between husbands and wives, we actually planned to raise our kids together on my dad's place. She didn't go to college to escape menial drudgery; she went to act on a phrase in her patriarchal blessing about seeking all the education to which she could attain. So she attained two years' worth, and, at age twenty, she attained Milton Murdock, from Ely, Nevada—a six-foot-two, 230-pound ex-linebacker with a head full of thick hair, a white-toothed smile, and a surgery scar on each kneecap. When they met, he was eight months home from his mission and only recently cut from BYU's spring tryouts.

"You think I'd work like a dog to come back from two blown knees—wear ankle weights every day for two years in Korea—if I didn't think I was *meant* to play Cougar football?"

He asked this question of Eden on their first date. Back in Ely, he said, when he was making most of the tackles for the White Pine Bobcats, everybody called him Mighty Milt. But not anymore. Licking such a wound, he was bound to have looked handsome, easy to see as the one intended for her. Maybe that's when she said that with faith and hard work, the sky's the limit. And maybe that's when he looked in her eyes and decided the Lord might have something besides football in mind for Milt Murdock. Whatever happened on that date, it happened two weeks before a big UPS truck delivered three pallets of goat-whey lotion at the top of the concrete stairway of his basement apartment.

The new plan was to make millions selling the lotion, then retire on the interest and serve the Lord in ways only rich people can—sponsoring scholarships, fundraising to fight poverty and disease, having buildings named after them. If goat whey caught on, he wouldn't have much time for college, so, with only two semesters behind him, he dropped out.

But goat whey didn't catch on. Nor did tap-water filtering systems, nor night-crawler sod stimulant, nor family survival kits in a bucket. Nor Therma-Zap. That's the last one I was privy to before I graduated and went home to Balford.

"Come with me, Ever." Milt was hungry for the per-head "bonus" he would earn taking guests to a Therma-Zap recruiting "seminar." He invited my roommates, too. But Tucker, long ago burned out on Amway, said no thanks. And Rolo, who mostly watched TV through four years' worth of evenings in Provo, suddenly had an appointment at the library. "Looks like it's just me and you," Milt said. "This might give you a whole new perspective."

What it gave me was the willies. Four or five overgroomed ex-missionaries in three-piece suits and tasseled dress shoes, bearing testimony of attic insulation in front of a hotel conference room full of penniless college guys. At the end of the show, the ringleader, the winner of last year's Hawaii trip, trotted in from wherever he'd been hiding and introduced himself as Val. He parted his hair slightly off-center and wore contact lenses with a turquoise tint. Blinking with well-practiced sincerity, he allowed there's nothing wrong with digging ditch or pounding nails all summer, for five or six bucks an hour—*if* a person is satisfied with that.

"But, gentlemen," he asked after a long, dramatic pause, "is that going to satisfy *you*?"

No!

"Do you think the Lord *wants* you earning peanuts when you could make ten or fifteen thousand dollars—in one summer?"

NO-OOO!

You would've thought we were rallying for the virtue of sisters and mothers—not foam pellets. And eight long years after Mighty Milt Murdock made one last goal-line stand, on knees already ruined for college ball, he could join again in thumbs-upping and whistling.

"*Go-ooo Therma-Zap!*"

He left Eden seven months pregnant with their third child, went out to Portland and shared a flat with several of the two hundred guys who, like him, had stampeded to the sign-up line. They just knew they were meant to make all those thousands—a *minimum* for can-do self-starters with stick-to-itiveness, promised the fast-blinking Val, who saw the world through turquoise lenses.

Milt lasted a month going door to door, had to borrow for a bus ticket to get home.

Go Therma-Zap.

⇒   ⇐

One night in March, a couple of years after I graduated and left Provo, Eden called me and confided that none of the schemes since Therma-Zap had turned out any better. Once upon a time, the sky might have been the limit, but not anymore. She was crying. To make rent, she explained, Milton managed the apartment complex they lived in. He did do that. He was a good guy, she assured me, and she loved him. But he wasn't the one begging day-old bread from a bakery, lining up, week after week, for government surplus honey and cheese and powdered milk. He wasn't the one hauling babies around on two different paper routes. "I tell you, Ever," she said, "I never thought life would be this way."

She blew her nose and apologized, said she had to tell somebody and was tired of listening to our mother harp on how Milt should have gotten an education like Bennett and Kayle, how a coaching job—or any job at all—would look pretty darned good about now. "Maybe I should have encouraged him more in that direction," Eden said. "But he was so *convinced* that this was what he's supposed to do. How do you argue with that?"

That was as good a question for Never-Ever as for Milton Murdock. In a lifetime, what *is* enough? At the time of Eden's phone call, Grandpa Warner had been dead over twenty years. I sort of wished I could phone *him* and ask if it was going to matter in the hereafter whether I held on to the land he grubbed out of sagebrush. Godwin, Godwin, and Son.

"I don't know why I'm such a boob tonight," Eden said. Then, after a pause, she said she missed the fields in April, green with new grain. She wondered if we were busy getting ready for planting. She hesitated. She said they were coming for a visit the next week—was there any chance Dad and I could use Milt on the farm for a while?

"Does Milt know you're talking to me about this?"

"I'm going to tell him," she said.

After our good-byes, I thought how strange life is. I loved the farm. I did. On the last leg home from the Philippines, in a prop plane from Denver to Cody, I choked up when Heart

Mountain came on the horizon and I could place again the little patch of Wyoming I grew up on. And a few years later, after my own graduation ceremony, I was antsy to get home. My folks were looking forward to dinner and a movie and a second night in a motel, which was as close to a vacation as they ever got. Yet, at the time, I saw my offer to drive through the night as a great generosity.

But home for the long stretch was different from home between semesters of school. Not so much better or worse— just nothing within the range of my foresight. When Eden called, I was already headed into my third season using my Ag Econ degree to drive worn-out, cableless tractors in forty-degree weather. Those hours breathing diesel exhaust went a long way toward dispelling the charm of wind, of living by myself in a trailer house above a milkweed patch, of sitting every Sunday on the back pew with Widow Penroy and her bachelor son Hewell.

And riding the tractor seat only magnified the charm of the BYU life I was in such a hurry to leave. With each hour roller-harrowing in lonely fields below Balford, college girls got prettier, classrooms warmer, and Provo skies bluer. I found myself envying my old roommate Rolo, of all people. He had finally gotten up off the couch and was going for a master's degree—in business administration. Unbeknownst to him, his chosen path met with my mother's hearty approval. On top of that, he was dating the profoundly beautiful cousin of my other roommate, Tucker. Through many hours of engine throb and self-pity, I wished for another of Tucker's many fair and marriageable cousins to come loping toward my tractor on a white unicorn, its hooves unmuddied by tilled ground. The Lord must wonder sometimes if we don't actually relish discontent.

At breakfast, a couple of days after Eden's call, my dad and I disclosed our intention to offer Milt a job. My mother looked up from her oatmeal and said, "Are you both out of your minds?"

I said, "It's got to beat goat lotion and attic insulation."

"Ever," she said, "I'm not sure farming beats anything."

I never told her what went on in my head while I drove tractor. She would have said, "See what I told you?" And she would have missed the point. Dreaming bluer skies didn't make a case against farming; it made a case against dreaming bluer skies.

True enough, I hadn't predicted life with any accuracy to brag about. But my mother hadn't either. While she rightly foresaw her own satisfaction with her two oldest daughters' full and happy lives, she didn't foresee its underside: the envy hidden amid her fuss at every new bounty made possible by optometry and law; the cheerfully swallowed hurt when her own daughters laughed at her methods—scraping swill into a bucket perched *right there* on the clothes dryer, baking with *lard*, stretching a can of tuna to its *utmost limits* with half a jar of mayonnaise; the smiling weariness at my sisters' overdone praise for their modest upbringing—*Oh, Mother, how did you ever do it with just one bathroom and that old car?*

It was odd, but in such moments my mother actually took up for the farm. "We made out all right," she said. "You two look like you survived just fine." At such times, she actually cast me as an ally. "Your brother here came back," she said. "He must not have minded the life so much—did you, Ever?"

Still, my mother didn't want Eden to come back; she wouldn't go that far in taking up for the farm. But her worries about our Milt strategy were wasted. He wasn't the least bit interested in the munificence of Tolbert and Ever Godwin.

"You mean like *farm* work?" he asked, sitting across from me and my dad at the kitchen table. "With you guys?"

Now that it was clear how he felt about our work, we kindly asked what sort of work he *was* partial to. He didn't hedge at all, at least not in the way you might expect of a guy who hadn't drawn more than half a dozen paychecks in a row in almost eight years of marriage. "I want to succeed," he said resolutely, parroting one of the motivational hucksters whose books and tapes he was always pushing on my folks.

My dad told him that a lot of life depended on how you looked at success and failure. And, in my tender wisdom, I said the wealth promised in his patriarchal blessing might have to be read as something due a lot later in life. Or maybe it couldn't be read as money at all. Milt had never seen my dad as anything but a good old farm guy and my mother as an able meat-and-potatoes cook, but he respected them. So out of that respect, he made a show of at least considering my dad's point. But mine? In one ear and out the other.

Then, very politely, with a conviction Therma-Zap Val would be proud of, Milt said to both of us, "I think when the Lord says material success, he means material success—sometime in normal mortality."

⇒ ⇐

So Milton and I ruined my mother's clean sweep of success and fulfillment in her children.

Nevertheless, by the fourth year of farming with my dad, I could have stood in somebody's cornfield and checked off a good many of my own promised blessings. Tillage and reaping—I had that one for sure, all day, every day. The biggest one missing from that season of my life was the lovely daughter of Zion. And without that one, I couldn't see how my promised parenthood would come to pass.

"It's not a new problem," my dad said on another cold March evening, after another day of windy tractor work, over another supper of pork chops and gravy. "Look at Isaac and Rebekah; look at Jacob and Rachel. Many a great man has had to go beyond his native borders to find a worthy helpmate." He kept his eyes averted from my mother, whose spatula was sliding two biscuits from a hot cookie sheet onto his plate. "For that matter," he said, with no change of tone, "look at Tolbert and Mina—he had to go all the way from Balford to Cowley."

It took a moment for that last statement to register with my mother. When it did, she clucked her tongue at my dad's effrontery and muttered, "Many a great man!" But for an instant, with her spatula poised above the millionth biscuit of her life, she smiled.

I was no great man. I lived in a single-wide trailer above a milkweed patch. I knew who was at the bottom of the chain and where to direct my troubleshooting. In counseling Milt Murdock, I was more than willing to delay *his* blessing to some distant point. Yet I was hoping to claim my own a little earlier than that. And a hundred times a day I invoked his logic to justify that claim: When the Lord says a wife, I think he means a wife—sometime in normal mortality.

And so he did.

"You're going where?" That's what my future wife's father said when she announced she was coming to Wyoming, to teach history at Cody Community College. Like any father in his shoes, he naturally wondered why Jen had applied for something in the boonies when hometown Fresno and other nearby California places had all kinds of schools where someone with her degree could teach. Jen didn't know—until her other possibilities evaporated. But she still didn't know why Cody was the one that *didn't* evaporate. We hadn't known each other very long when she told me all this. "Come to find out," she said with less-than-romantic resignation, "Cody is pretty close to Balford. And Balford—a spot on the globe I never otherwise would have had the pleasure of knowing—is where *you* happen to live."

A farmer! Oh my!

Even in my most maudlin white-unicorn moments, I could not imagine my future mother-in-law uttering that line in her Fresno kitchen while talking into her Fresno telephone, at least not with any enthusiasm. As part of my marriage proposal, I told Jen about the tillage and reaping, wanted her to see the same inevitability I did. She said I was confusing a blessing with a plan and forgetting who was responsible for each. She said it sounded like I wanted mortality to be neater than it could be. She said maybe I was trying to hold the Lord accountable for making *me*, Everett Godwin, accountable. Then, after a long pause, she said the Lord might have guided her to Balford, but he wasn't forcing anything. "What you've done with your life so far is your choice," she said, "and whether I do it with you from here on is mine."

⇒   ⇐

When my mother died a few weeks ago, my sisters and their families of course came home for the funeral. After the dedication of the grave and the Relief Society meal at church, we all went back to our house on its half-acre lot in Balford, the house Jen and I moved into when I lost six hundred acres of farm land and pasture. Our children and grandchildren had the run of the yard and house, except for the living room. There, on the sofa and loveseat, my sisters sat close to their husbands. Jen and I sat in kitchen chairs.

"Ever miss the old farm . . . Ever?" Kayle Lowder asked, to break the somber silence. Even in mourning, he was fascinated with my name. He said he thought of me every time he came across a client christened with something unusual. Eventide. Glory. Rainbow. "I kid you not," he said. "That's what got signed on the dotted line."

After a moment, Eden looked at me and asked, "*Do* you miss the farm?"

The quiet in the room was like a lid I didn't want to lift.

After a moment, Afton Rae said, "I know I miss it." Then she said, "It was such a good way to grow up. I wanted so much for our grandchildren to *see* that way of life."

"Yeah," said Milt, who lately was managing a takeout barbeque restaurant in American Fork, Utah, and selling animated movies of Book of Mormon stories, "but it's sure a tough way to make a buck."

Bennett, who has made an awful lot of bucks checking people's eyes in his string of optometry clinics in Denver, nodded with a very reflective look on his face.

"I always just assumed," Leona said, "that you'd end up farming Daddy's place, that we'd keep it in the family. Doesn't your patriarchal blessing say that?"

The room fell quiet again. We had all lived beyond the halfway mark of our lives. As spouse or parent or human being, every person there had known some piece of the mortal mix—if not money problems, then something else. Sickness and setback, a wayward child or two, shaken faith. Even a cleft palate.

But then Jen, who remembers history better than most and always gives faith its due, said, "He did farm it—for twelve years."

⟅   ⟅

A week or so after my sisters went back to their lives, I found myself driving over what used to be my dad's farm but is a farm no longer. I went, not on Weed and Pest business, but to help with a service project for a couple from church who moved here from Lansing, Michigan. It was the first time I had made myself go back since I lost the place five years ago. Turning down the properly graded and graveled lane was like launching a tour of my own failure. I found myself trying to decide where my mother's raspberry patch might have been, but there were no toeholds for memory. Barns, bins, burn barrels, chicken house, outhouse, our house—everything was gone except the land. And it was cut up into lots for new-home units, one of which now belonged to the nice couple from Lansing. Their big brick house was all but finished; they just needed help landscaping the sizable yard.

"Before we get started," the wife said, using the balustrade of her front porch as a rostrum, "I just want you all to know this house—and your help—is an answer to our prayers." She said her patriarchal blessing promised she would raise her children in a place of peace and beauty, away from the dangers of city life. "We feel we've found that here in Balford," she said. She looked then to her husband, who made everybody laugh when he pointed to two approaching trucks and said it looked like it was time to work for some of that peace and beauty. He asked if we'd gotten the word to bring wheelbarrows and shovels and rakes. Soon enough we knew why. One truck was full of rock, and the other, potted sagebrush.

≡   ≡

Midafternoon of a warm day in June, thirty years ago, Patriarch J. Guyman LeGrand stood behind a ladder-back chair in his parlor, on two spots of carpet worn in the shape of his Sunday shoes. At that moment, he was alive and lucid and, as he put it, healthy as a horse on oats and beet molasses. A few hours later he was dead.

He and Sister LeGrand had been married seventy-five years. In her sudden loneliness, she told many people, including my mother, the story of his last hours. Even after Sister LeGrand died herself, that story nagged me; I wondered if she had blamed me, if maybe she thought giving my blessing had something to do with that afternoon being her husband's last. But, strangely enough, since my mother's death, that same story has been a comfort.

After my blessing, after my parents and I drove off, Brother J. Guyman returned the ladder-back chair to its place in the corner, put away the tape recorder in his little closet-office, and changed into a pair of blue cotton coveralls. Then he went outside to move the lawn sprinkler. Sister LeGrand said he looked at her begonias for the longest time. He finally came back in, read scriptures, and announced he was going to lie down a minute before evening prayer and his Sunday supper of bread and milk. A little later she set the bowl and pitcher and loaf on the table, then peeled and sliced a peach the way he liked it. "Papa," she called, "you don't want the milk to get warm." Only when she had called a third time did the dread come over her.

When J. Guyman retired from the sugar-beet factory, the bosses gave him a nice pocket watch. Lying in his blue coveralls, on the narrow bed in their cracker box of a room, he was clutching that watch in one of his papyrus hands and staring with the most serene amazement at something through and far beyond the ceiling. After all those years of inspired foresight, what fell under the sweep of his eye there at the end? Something beyond tillage and reaping. I'm sure of that. Lately, riding farmers' back roads, I imagine my mother looking and looking in the same direction. And whatever she sees, whatever lies in front of her now, it is enough.

ACKNOWLEDGMENTS

I AM GRATEFUL TO GREGG HEITSCHMIDT FOR EDITING this volume. Many an improvement, big and little, can be attributed to his sharp eye and insight. And editing was only his most recent help. Long before these stories made it to the page in their present form, he listened to me speak of them. Only he knows which labor required more forbearance.

ABOUT THE AUTHOR

D ARIN COZZENS GREW UP IN RALSTON, WYOMING.
After serving as a missionary in Ecuador, he earned a B.A.
from Brigham Young University, an M.F.A. from the University
of North Carolina–Greensboro, and a Ph.D. from Oklahoma
State University. He has been a semifinalist for the Ohio State
University Press Prize in Short Fiction and a finalist for both
the Iowa Short Fiction Awards and Sarabande's Mary McCarthy
Prize in Short Fiction. He and his wife are the parents of four
children and live in Dobson, North Carolina, where he teaches
at Surry Community College.

www.ingramcontent.com/pod-product-compliance
Lightning Source LLC
Chambersburg PA
CBHW031428250626

47155CB00004B/1662